THE CHILD'S WORLD®

ENCYCLOPEDIA
of BASEBALL

TY COBB

VOLUME 1: HANK AARON THROUGH CY YOUNG AWARD

By James Buckley, Jr., David Fischer, Jim Gigliotti, and Ted Keith

KEY TO SYMBOLS

Throughout *The Child's World® Encyclopedia of Baseball*, you'll see these symbols. They'll give you a quick clue pointing to each entry's general subject area.

Active player   *Baseball word or phrase*   *Hall of Fame*   *Miscellaneous*   *Ballpark*   *Team*

The Child's World
www.childsworld.com

Published in the United States of America by The Child's World®
1980 Lookout Drive, Mankato, MN 56003-1705
800-599-READ • www.childsworld.com

ACKNOWLEDGMENTS

The Child's World®: Mary Berendes, Publishing Director

Produced by Shoreline Publishing Group LLC
President / Editorial Director: James Buckley, Jr.
Cover Design: Kathleen Petelinsek, The Design Lab
Interior Design: Tom Carling, carlingdesign.com
Assistant Editors: Jim Gigliotti, Zach Spear

Cover Photo Credits: Focus on Baseball (main); National Baseball Hall of Fame Library (inset).
Interior Photo Credits: AP/Wide World: 4, 8, 10, 11, 14, 15, 16, 18, 23, 24, 25, 34, 38, 40, 44, 49, 50, 56, 67, 68, 74, 75, 77, 80, 81, 83. Corbis: 7, 52, 53, 62, 71, 82; Focus on Baseball: 9, 12, 17, 19, 21, 26, 27, 31, 32, 33, 39, 41, 43, 48, 51, 54, 57, 58, 59, 60, 61, 63, 65, 66, 69, 70, 73, 78, 79; Getty Images: 45; Library of Congress: 46; Al Messerschmidt: 5, 6, 35, 36, 42, 55, 64, 72; National Baseball Hall of Fame Library: 29, 36, 40.

LIBRARY OF CONGRESS CATALOG-IN-PUBLICATION DATA

The Child's World encyclopedia of baseball / by James Buckley, Jr. ... [et al.].
    p. cm. – (The Child's World encyclopedia of baseball)
 Includes index.
 ISBN 978-1-60253-167-3 (library bound : alk. paper)–ISBN 978-1-60253-168-0 (library bound : alk. paper)–ISBN 978-1-60253-169-7 (library bound : alk. paper)–ISBN 978-1-60253-170-3 (library bound : alk. paper)–ISBN 978-1-60253-171-0 (library bound : alk. paper)
 1. Baseball–United States–Encyclopedias, Juvenile. I. Buckley, James, 1963- II. Child's World (Firm) III. Title. IV. Series.

GV867.5.C46 2009
796.3570973–dc22

2008039461

Yankees great Yogi Berra.

PEOPLE HAVE BEEN PLAYING BASEBALL, America's national, pastime, for more than 150 years, so we needed a lot of room to do it justice! The five big volumes of *The Child's World' Encyclopedia of Baseball* hold as much as we could squeeze in about this favorite sport.

The Babe. The Say-Hey Kid. The Iron Horse. The Splendid Splinter. Rapid Robert. Hammerin' Hank. You'll read all about these great players of yesterday. You'll also learn about your favorite stars of today: Pujols, Jeter, Griffey, Soriano, Santana, Manny, and Big Papi. How about revisiting some of baseball's most memorable plays and games? The Shot Heard 'Round the World. The Catch. The Grand-Slam Single. You'll find all of these–and more.

Have a favorite big-league team? They're all here, with a complete history for each team that includes its all-time record.

Ever wonder what it means to catch a can of corn, hit a dinger, or use a fungo? Full coverage of baseball's unique and colorful terms will let you understand and speak the language as if you were born to it.

This homegrown sport is a part of every child's world, and our brand-new encyclopedia makes read-ing about it almost as fun as playing it!

Cardinals ace Chris Carpenter.

Contents: Volume 1: Hank Aaron » Cy Young Award

Alexander, Pete

Pete Alexander was one of the dominant pitchers of the 1910s and 1920s. He also was known by his given first name of Grover, or by his full name of Grover Cleveland Alexander.

In 20 big-league seasons with three franchises beginning in 1911, Alexander won 373 games. That equals fellow Hall-of-Famer Christy Mathewson for the best in National League history and for the third-best among all pitchers in big-league history. Alexander won eight times on Opening

■ *Alexander was a Cardinals' World Series hero.*

Day (tied for second all-time), and won 20 or more games nine times and 30 or more games three times.

For all his accomplishments, however, Alexander is best known for one moment late in his career. It came while he was pitching for the St. Louis Cardinals against the New York Yankees in Game Seven of the 1926 World Series. Alexander had already started, and won, two games earlier in the Series, including Game Six. But he entered the final game in relief in the seventh inning with the bases loaded, two out, and the Cardinals leading 3–2. In one of the most memorable moments in baseball history, Alexander struck out future Hall-of-Famer Tony Lazzeri to preserve the lead. He shut down the Yankees over the final two innings, too, and the Cardinals won the World Series.

Alexander overcame many obstacles along the way to his Hall-of-Fame induction in 1938. He missed most of the 1918 season while serving in the military during World War I. The experience left him deaf in one ear. Alexander also suffered from epilepsy and alcoholism.

All-American Girls Professional Baseball League

The All-American Girls Professional Baseball League, or AAGPBL, was a World War II-era softball and baseball league for women.

Aaron, Hank

Hank Aaron stood as baseball's home-run king for more than three decades, beginning in 1974. That year, he slugged home run No. 715 off Los Angeles' Al Downing to surpass Babe Ruth's career mark.

Aaron was not a typical modern, muscular slugger. Instead, he stood just 6 feet and weighed 180 pounds. But his wrists were amazingly quick, and when he drove them through the hitting zone, they helped him launch 755 home runs in a 23-year Major League career that began in 1954. Although he never hit more than 45 homers in any season, he belted at least 24 in 19 consecutive years beginning in 1955.

Aaron was more than just a home-run hitter, though. He amassed 3,771 hits, batted .305 overall, and set a big-league record that still stands by driving in 2,297 runs in his career. He also stole 240 bases and won three Gold Gloves for his play in the outfield. He made the All-Star Game a record 25 times (there were two All-Star Games played each season from 1959 to 1962). He was inducted into the Hall of Fame in 1982. That year, he received votes on a remarkable 97.8 percent of the ballots.

■ *Aaron broke Babe Ruth's record with this homer.*

For many years, Aaron came first alphabetically on Major League Baseball's all-time roster of players, in addition to being tops on the all-time home-run chart. Aaron is second on both lists now. (For the record, David Aardsma is first alphabetically and Barry Bonds is the home-run king.)

"Hammerin' Hank," though, still remains one of the most popular players in the history of baseball.

All-Star Game

Major League Baseball's All-Star Game began in 1933. Arch Ward, the sports editor of the *Chicago Tribune*, came up with the idea as a way to boost attendance at his city's "Century of Progress" Expo, and to boost waning interest in baseball in the midst of the Great Depression.

The American League won that first game 4–2 at Chicago's Comiskey Park largely on the strength of a home run by the Yankees' Babe Ruth, who was near the end of his legendary career. Some 49,200 fans attended the game, which made it such a huge success that it became a yearly tradition. The game, which is sometimes called the "Midsummer Classic," has been held every season since, except for 1945. That year, World War II forced its cancellation. The leagues played twice each season from 1959 to 1962.

The starting lineups for the position players (everyone except the pitcher) in the All-Star Game are determined by fan voting. That tradition began in 1947, was suspended for 12 years beginning in 1958, and returned for good in 1970. The American League and National League managers are the men who guided their teams to the World Series the previous year. They choose pitchers and reserves. Each Major League team must be represented by at least one player.

Although baseball's All-Star Game remains the most popular of all sports' annual exhibitions, it doesn't have the status it once did. With the advent of interleague play, it is no longer such a novelty to see players from the different leagues playing on the same field. So Major League Baseball has tried to attract more attention again to the All-Star Game. In recent seasons, the league that wins the All-Star Game earns home-field advantage for its pennant winner when the World Series is played in October.

The N.L. entered the 2009 season with 41 all-time wins in the All-Star Game, while the American League had won 36 times, and two games ended in ties. But the American League had won six games in a row and was 11-0-1 in the last 12 meetings.

■ *All-Stars Barry Bonds and Cal Ripken Jr.*

With many big-league stars away fighting overseas in the war, baseball fans sought other places to watch their favorite sport. The AAGPBL helped fill the void and eventually became a big hit.

Cubs owner Philip K. Wrigley helped start the AAGPBL, which began as a softball league with four teams in the Midwest. But the league soon dropped softball in favor of baseball and rapidly grew in popularity. The game was played on a smaller diamond, with 72 feet (22 m) between the bases instead of 90 (27 m), but otherwise was the same game that the men played.

At its height in the late 1940s, the AAGPBL's 10 teams played in front of more than 900,000 fans one season. But with the men back from the war and more big-league games on television, interest in the AAGPBL quickly fell. By 1952, only six teams remained; two years later, the league closed its doors.

Allen, Mel

Mel Allen was the radio voice of the New York Yankees for 26 seasons beginning in 1939. In that time, the Yankees were the most powerful team in baseball, and Allen became the most recognizable announcer in baseball.

Allen's friendly and unique voice–plus catchphrases such as "How about that!"–made him a fan favorite, not only in New York, but also around the country. Baseball fans outside New York City got to know his work through his 22 seasons as a World Series announcer and 24 seasons as the All-Star Game announcer. In the 1980s, he also became the host of a popular national television show called *This Week in Baseball*. By that time, he also had returned to the Yankees to do cable TV broadcasts.

In 1978, Allen and Red Barber became the first men voted into a special broadcasters wing of the Baseball Hall of Fame.

Alomar, Roberto

Roberto Alomar was a 12-time All-Star second baseman who played for seven big-league teams in a 17-season career from 1988 to 2004.

Alomar is the younger brother of former Major League catcher Sandy Alomar Jr., and the son of former big-league infielder Sandy Alomar Sr. Roberto was only 20 years old when he made his debut with the San Diego Padres in 1988. Two years later, he earned the first of his All-Star selections, which came in 12 consecutive years.

Alomar developed into one of the top run-producing middle infielders in baseball in the 1990s and early 2000s. He hit 20 or more homers three times, drove in at least 100 runs twice, and scored more than 100 runs in six seasons. He had a career batting average of .300, including a .336 mark for Cleveland in 2001. He also overcame fielding troubles early in his career to become a

■ *Alomar was a top player for several teams.*

10-time Gold Glove second baseman. And he helped the Blue Jays win back-to-back World Series in 1992 and 1993.

Alomar can be elected to the Hall of Fame beginning in 2010.

Alston, Walter

Walter Alston was the manager of the Dodgers for 23 seasons from 1954—when the club was still in Brooklyn—through 1976. In that time, he guided the franchise to seven pennants and four World Series victories. His teams won 2,040 games in all, which still ranks ninth on baseball's all-time list. He was inducted into the Hall of Fame in 1983.

Before Alston took over as the Dodgers' manager, Brooklyn had won five National League pennants in 13 seasons. Each time, however, the club fell to the local-rival New York Yankees in the World Series. In just his second season at the helm, though, Alston guided the Dodgers to a thrilling, seven-game victory over the Yankees in the 1955 World Series. It was the only championship ever for the Dodgers in Brooklyn. The team moved to Los Angeles in 1958. Alston went on to lead the L.A. Dodgers to World Series titles in 1959, 1963, and 1965.

Alston was noted as much for his soft-spoken and polite manner as for the success his teams had. Several of his players, including Gil Hodges, Tommy Lasorda, Bobby Valentine, and Don Zimmer, followed in his footsteps as Major League managers. Lasorda succeeded Alston as the Dodgers' manager in 1977.

American Association

The American Association was a major league that existed from 1882 to 1891. It initially was formed in response to the National League's refusal to allow baseball to be played on Sundays or for beer to be sold at the games.

Because the American Association sold beer at its games, and because several owners also had a stake in breweries, it was referred to by its opponents as the "Beer and Whiskey League." But the new league did well, and several current National League teams—including the Reds, Dodgers, Pirates, and Cardinals—trace their roots to the American Association.

The American Association started as a six-team league in 1882, had as many as 12 teams two years later, and included eight franchises in its final season. The league ended in 1891 when four of its teams jumped to the older National League.

Beginning with the American Association's very first season in 1882, its champion met the National League champion in a series of postseason exhibition games. Two years later, the winners of the two leagues met in an official series to determine the champion of baseball. Those series are sometimes referred to as the "19th Century World Series," although modern World Series history officially began when the American League and National League winners first played in 1903.

American League

The American League was founded by Ban Johnson as an eight-team league in 1901 to compete directly with the established National League. Today, it is a 14-team league split into three divisions.

The American League plays by the same rules as the National League, with the notable exception of the designated-hitter rule (see "Designated Hitter"), which was instituted in 1973. Because the American League is 25 years younger than the National League, it is still sometimes called the "Junior Circuit."

■ *The White Sox (top) and Tigers are longtime A.L. teams.*

A.L. founder Johnson was the president of the Western League, the strongest of the minor leagues, in the mid-1890s. When the N.L. cut back from 12 teams to 8 at the turn of the century, he decided the time was right to start a second major league.

In 1900, Johnson placed several teams in existing National League cities and

■ *Boston celebrated an ALCS title in 2007.*

renamed the Western League the American League. It still competed as a minor league that season. One year later, though, the American League declared itself a major league and began a full-scale bidding war with the National League for the services of big-league players.

Almost from the start, the American League competed on a par with the National League, both in terms of level of play and fan attention. By 1903, the two leagues agreed to have their champions meet at the end of the season; thus, the World Series was born. In 1904, the N.L.-champion New York Giants refused to play the A.L.-champion Boston Pilgrims. The World Series resumed in 1905, however, and was played every year until a players' strike wiped out the 1994 event.

American League Championship Series (ALCS)

The American League Championship Series, or ALCS, is the best-of-seven series (the first team to four victories wins) that determines the A.L.'s entry in the World Series. The ALCS is played between the two teams that win the league's Division Series.

The ALCS began in 1969, when the American League split into two divisions (East and West) for the first time. From 1969 to 1984, the Championship Series was best-of-five (the first team to three victories wins). In 1985, it became a best-of-seven series.

The Baltimore Orioles won each of the first three ALCS. The New York Yankees have won it the most times, with nine series victories entering 2009.

American League Division Series (ALDS)

The American League Division Series, or ALDS, is the opening round of the A.L. playoffs. It includes four teams: the three division winners (East, Central, and West) and the non-division winner with the best record (the wild-card team). In the ALDS, the first-place team with the best record plays the wild-card team, and the other two division winners play each other. Two teams from the same division can't meet in the ALDS, though, so sometimes the first-place team with the second-best record plays the wild-card team.

The two ALDS matchups are best-of-five games. The first team to win three games advances to the next round, which is the American League Championship Series (ALCS).

The ALDS officially was going to start in 1994, when the American League expanded from two to three divisions and was set to include a wild-card team for the first time. But because of a players' strike that year that cancelled the postseason, the ALDS did not actually begin until 1995. In

■ *Troy Percival celebrates at the 2002 ALDS.*

1981, another players' strike resulted in a split season that added an extra round of playoffs. The first round that year is included in all-time ALDS results and records.

Anaheim Angels

Anaheim Angels is the name under which the Los Angeles Angels of Anaheim (see that entry in Volume III) played from 1997 through 2004.

The franchise began play as the Los Angeles Angels in 1961. In 1965, the club changed its name to the California Angels, and the next season moved out of Los

■ *Anderson's teams won three World Series.*

Angeles to Anaheim, California. In 1997, the team changed again, this time to the Anaheim Angels. In 2005, although the club remained in Anaheim, the team name changed once more. This time, it officially became the Los Angeles Angels of Anaheim. However, the team is more commonly called simply the Los Angeles Angels.

Anderson, Sparky

Sparky Anderson was one of the most successful baseball managers of all time. In 26 big-league seasons beginning in 1970, Anderson won 2,194 games, which still ranked fifth on Major League Base-

ball's career list through 2008. He is one of only two men (Tony LaRussa is the other) to win a World Series in both the American League and the National League.

Anderson, whose real first name is George, managed most of his career with the Detroit Tigers (1979–1995). But he is perhaps best known for his years in Cincinnati. In nine seasons from 1970 to 1978, he guided the "Big Red Machine" to four National League pennants, including back-to-back World Series championships in 1975 and 1976. Cincinnati's seven-game victory over the Boston Red Sox for the 1975 championship is considered one of the greatest World Series ever.

Eight seasons later, Anderson's Detroit team got off to the best start in big-league history, winning 35 of its first 40 games. The Tigers went on to win the World Series in five games over the San Diego Padres.

Anderson, who was recognizable for his head of white hair, was popular with his players, fans, and the media. He was one of the first baseball managers to extensively rely on his bullpen, which earned him the nickname "Captain Hook" (because he so quickly pulled, or "hooked," his pitchers from games).

A former infielder who played one season in the Majors with Philadelphia in 1959, Anderson was inducted into the National Baseball Hall of Fame as a manager in 2000.

Anson, Cap

Cap Anson is often considered the greatest hitter of the 19th century. He played 22 seasons for the Chicago franchise in the National League beginning in 1876 and batted .339 for his career. His 3,081 career hits made him the first big leaguer to surpass the magical 3,000 mark (although pre-1900 figures are not always consistent, and some historians give that credit to Honus Wagner, who was the first man to reach 3,000 hits in the post-1900 era).

Before joining the Chicago White Stockings–they were called the Chicago Colts beginning in 1890–in the first year of the National League's existence, Anson was a star for five seasons in the National Association. The National Association was the highest level of play at the time. In 27 years of pro ball, Anson hit better than .300 a remarkable 24 times. He won a pair of National League batting titles, with the first coming when he hit .399 in 1881.

Anson also was Chicago's player-manager beginning in 1879. He led the club to five National League titles in seven seasons beginning in 1880. At one time or another, Anson played every position for Chicago, even pitching three times in his career. He primarily was a first baseman, though.

Anson became so associated with the Chicago franchise that after he retired as both a player and a manager following the 1897 season, sportswriters began calling the club the "Orphans." The team did not become the Cubs, as they are still known today, until 1903.

Aparicio, Luis

In 18 big-league seasons beginning in 1956, Luis Aparicio batted a modest .262. He never hit more than 10 home runs in one year and never drove in more than 61 runs. But his value to the three A.L. clubs for which he played was so great in the field and on the base paths that he was inducted into the Hall of Fame in 1984.

continued on page 17

■ *Aparicio ended his Hall-of-Fame career with Boston.*

Arizona Diamondbacks

The Arizona Diamondbacks joined the National League as an expansion team in 1998—and it didn't take them long to make their mark on baseball history. The Diamondbacks won the World Series in just their fourth season of existence in 2001. That was the fastest path to a championship for any expansion team in baseball history.

■ *Webb has been Arizona's ace since 2003.*

From the beginning, though, it was obvious that the Diamondbacks were not an ordinary expansion team. Arizona's first squad featured several good players who were in the middle of excellent careers. It was not the usual rag-tag collection of aging veterans and youngsters trying to make a name for themselves that ordinarily make up a first-year club.

Instead, players such as third baseman Matt Williams, first baseman Travis Lee, shortstop Jay Bell, and center fielder Devon White all slugged 20 or more home runs for the Diamondbacks in 1998. Andy Benes was an ace starting pitcher, and Gregg Olson was a proven closer.

Manager Buck Showalter's team won 65 games that first year—not bad for an expansion team, but only a hint of what was to come. The next season, Arizona signed free-agent pitcher Randy Johnson. At 6 feet 10 inches tall and with a steely glare—oh, and a 100 mile-per-hour (160 km-per-hour) fastball—that intimidates even the best hitters, he is one of the most imposing pitchers ever.

In his first season with the Diamondbacks, Johnson won 17 games, struck out 364 batters, and earned the first of four consecutive Cy Young Awards as the best pitcher in the National League. More importantly, Arizona won 100 games and the N.L. West. No other expansion team had made the playoffs in just its second season.

Two seasons later, though, there was no stopping Arizona. By then, starting pitcher Curt Schilling and manager Bob Brenly had been added. Schilling teamed with Johnson to give the team one of the best righty-lefty punches in recent baseball history. And Brenly was a welcome change from Showalter, whose strict ways had upset players.

Johnson, the left-hander, won 21 games while striking out 372 batters and compiling an ERA of 2.49. Schilling, the right-hander, won 22 games while striking out 293 batters and compiling an ERA of 2.98. On offense, Gonzalez slugged 57 home runs.

After winning the National League playoffs, Arizona played in a dramatic World Series against the powerful New York Yankees. With the series tied at three games each, Arizona entered the bottom of the ninth inning of Game Seven trailing by a score of 2–1. The Yankees had Mariano Rivera, their great closer, on the mound. But first baseman Mark Grace opened the inning with a single. After an error

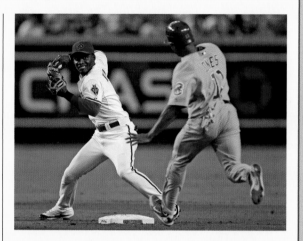

■ *Orlando Hudson turns two for Arizona.*

and a force play, shortstop Tony Womack doubled in the tying run. Second baseman Craig Counsell was hit by a pitch, bringing up Gonzalez with the bases loaded.

In one of the most dramatic moments in World Series history, Gonzalez looped a single into left-center field. Jay Bell scored from third base with the winning run. The Diamondbacks were world champions.

Arizona has had its ups and downs since then. It won only 51 games in 2004, but by 2007 had won another division title, led by pitcher Brandon Webb (who won the Cy Young Award in 2006). With Webb in the rotation, the Diamondbacks are ready to strike again.

ARIZONA DIAMONDBACKS

LEAGUE: **NATIONAL**

DIVISION: **WEST**

YEAR FOUNDED: **1998**

CURRENT COLORS: **RED AND GOLD**

STADIUM (CAPACITY): **CHASE FIELD (49,033)**

ALL-TIME RECORD (THROUGH 2008): **900–882**

WORLD SERIES TITLES (MOST RECENT): **1 (2001)**

■ *Sadaharu Oh is an Asian baseball legend.*

Asia, Baseball in

Baseball has been played in Japan since the game first was introduced there in the 1870s by a visiting American professor at Tokyo University. The sport rapidly grew until it rivaled even the national sport of sumo wrestling in popularity.

Today, most Asian nations field national teams that are governed by the Baseball Federation of Asia. The Japanese team won the first World Baseball Classic in 2006; the team from South Korea finished third.

A team from Japan first won the Little League World Series in 1967. From 1969 to 1996, Taiwan dominated the Little League World Series, winning 17 times. A team from South Korea won back-to-back Little League titles in 1984 and 1985.

Major League players and teams have toured in Japan since the Chicago White Sox and New York Giants played a series of exhibitions there in 1913. In 2000, the Chicago Cubs and the New York Mets played Major League Baseball's first regular-season game outside of North America when they met in the season opener in the Tokyo Dome.

The first Japanese professional team was formed in 1920; in 1936, the Japanese Pro-Baseball League was formed. It eventually split into two leagues: the Central League and the Pacific League.

To Americans of the 20th century, the best-known Japanese star was slugger Sadaharu Oh. He belted a pro-record 868 home runs for the Yomiuri Giants from 1959 to 1980. In recent years, however, several former Japanese pros have made their mark in Major League Baseball, including pitcher Hideo Nomo, outfielders Ichiro Suzuki and Hideki Matsui, and pitcher Daisuke Matsuzaka.

Born in Venezuela, Aparicio was a slick-fielding shortstop who first came up to the majors with the Chicago White Sox in 1956. He earned A.L. rookie-of-the-year honors after stealing 21 bases—the first of nine consecutive seasons that he led the league in that category. Two seasons later, in 1958, Aparicio was named an All-Star for the first of seven seasons in a row, and earned the first of his nine career Gold Gloves. In 1959, he swiped 56 bases for the White Sox' league champions.

Aparicio also played for the Orioles and Red Sox before leaving baseball at age 39 following the 1973 season. At the time of his retirement, he had played more games at shortstop (2,581) than anyone else in big-league history. He also held records for the most chances, assists, and double plays turned.

Appling, Luke

Hall-of-Famer Luke Appling made his big-league debut for the Chicago White Sox in 1930. By the next season, he was the club's regular starting shortstop. Except for one season (1944) and part of another (1945) when he was in the military during World War II, he kept the job until 1950. In 1969, White Sox fans voted him as the greatest player in club history.

Appling was an outstanding leadoff batter and often ranked among the top 10 in the American League in on-base percent-

age. His specialty was fouling off pitches after the opposing pitcher got two strikes on him. He would do that repeatedly until getting a hit or drawing a walk. (Reports say that he once fouled off 17 pitches in a row before hitting a triple.) That helped him bat .310 for his 20-season career. He had 2,749 hits and 1,302 bases on balls, both of which still rank among the top 50 among all players in big-league history.

In 1936, Appling hit a career-best .388 to earn the first of two career batting titles and the first of seven career All-Star selections. He went on to play 2,218 games at shortstop in his career. That total was the most in Major League history until Luis Aparicio, another White Sox player, came along. Appling joined the Hall of Fame in 1964.

Arizona Diamondbacks

Please see pages 14–15.

Assist

A player earns an assist when he makes a throw to another player that results in a putout. For example, when an outfielder throws to home plate and the catcher tags out the runner, the outfielder gets an assist. Every time a shortstop or other infielder picks up a grounder and throws to first base for the out, he gets an assist. In 1980, shortstop Ozzie Smith set a single-season record with 621 assists.

Atlanta Braves

The Braves have been based in three different cities and won a World Series title at each stop. Beginning in 1991, they had their best run. The Braves won 14 straight division titles, through 2005.

The Braves' history began in Boston in the National Association in 1871. They were called the Red Stockings then, and became the Red Caps when they joined the newly formed National League in 1876. They had various other nicknames, including Beaneaters (1883–1906), Doves (1907–1910), and Rustlers (1911) before becoming the Braves in 1912. Except for a period from 1936 to 1940, when the club was known as the Boston Bees, it has been the Braves ever since.

Behind players such as Hall-of-Famer Hugh Duffy, who hit an incredible .440 in 1894, Boston won eight pennants before the World Series era began in 1903. The team's first World Series win came in 1914.

After that, it was a long time before the Braves were good again. In 1948, Johnny Sain and Warren Spahn pitched Boston to the National League pennant. They were so good and got so little help from the club's other pitchers that a poem in a Boston paper coined the phrase, "Spahn and Sain and pray for rain" (that is, those two would pitch, and then fans hoped for days of rain delay so that that pair could pitch again!).

Boston lost the 1948 World Series to the Cleveland Indians, however. In 1953, the team moved to Milwaukee. Spahn, Lew Burdette, and third baseman Eddie Mathews were great players, but the biggest star of all in Milwaukee was Hank Aaron. He joined the club in 1954 and went on

■ *Braves ace Spahn shows off his famous form.*

to play 21 seasons for the Braves. In 1974, he became baseball's all-time home-run leader.

The 1957 Braves won the National League pennant and beat the Yankees in the World Series when Burdette tossed a shutout in Game Seven. The '58 squad also won the pennant, but lost to the Yankees in the World Series. In 1966, the team was on the move again—this time to Atlanta.

With stars such as outfielder Dale Murphy and pitcher Phil Niekro, the Braves had some good years in Atlanta but faltered in the late 1980s. But under Bobby Cox, who took over as the Braves' manager for the second time midway through 1990 (he also was the manager from 1978 to 1981), Atlanta was baseball's surprise team in 1991. The Braves came from behind to win the division.

A young pitching staff featuring starters Tom Glavine, John Smoltz, and Steve Avery set the Braves apart. Strong starting pitching—with Greg Maddux replacing Avery among the team's Big Three—would become the team's hallmark over the next decade.

Atlanta won the N.L. West again in 1992 and '93 (edging the Giants by one game in a thrilling race that was not decided until the final day), then moved to the N.L. East when Major League Baseball rearranged its teams in 1994.

All the Braves' regular-season success, however, did not carry over to the postseason. Despite the 14 division championships—including a club-record, 106-win season in 1998—Atlanta won the World Series championship only once. That came in 1995, when they beat the Cleveland Indians in an exciting six-game series in which five of the games were decided by one run.

Still, no matter how you look at it, 14 years is a long time. It's especially long in the modern world of sports, where players and coaches constantly come and go. But the Braves' run did not end until they slumped to a 79–83 record and a third-place finish in 2006. It was their first losing record since the 1990 season. Looks like it's time to start a new streak in Atlanta.

■ *Chipper Jones leads the Braves.*

ATLANTA BRAVES

LEAGUE: **NATIONAL**

DIVISION: **EAST**

YEAR FOUNDED: **1871**

CURRENT COLORS: **RED, BLUE, WHITE**

STADIUM (CAPACITY): **TURNER FIELD (50,096)**

ALL-TIME RECORD (THROUGH 2008): **9,768–9,807**

WORLD SERIES TITLES (MOST RECENT): **3 (1995)**

■ *Jimmy Rollins set a record for at-bats in 2007.*

Astrodome

The Astrodome was the home of the National League's Houston Astros from 1965 through 1999. In 2000, the team moved into its new home stadium, which is now called Minute Maid Park.

The Astrodome was nicknamed the "Eighth Wonder of the World" because it was the first multipurpose domed stadium. The Astrodome was also the home of football's Houston Oilers from 1968–1996.

The Astros played their home games on natural grass inside the Astrodome in their first season there. But when the grass died, the club turned to scientists to come up with an alternative surface. Their invention came to be known as AstroTurf.

At-bat

At-bat is an official statistic that is used to help determine a player's batting average and slugging percentage.

At-bats include the total number of times a player comes up to bat (a stat called "plate appearances"), minus the number of times that he walks, gets hit by a pitch, sacrifices, or is awarded first base on catcher's interference.

Batting average can then be figured by dividing a player's number of hits by his at-bats; slugging percentage is the number of total bases divided by at-bats.

Pete Rose is the career leader in at-bats with 14,503. Red Sox outfielder Doc Cramer set a record by leading the American League in at-bats seven times in his career. In 2007, Philadelphia shortstop Jimmy Rollins set a new all-time single-season record with 716 at-bats.

Atlanta Braves

Please see pages 18–19.

Attendance

Major League Baseball set an attendance record for the fourth consecutive season in 2007. More than 79.5 million people attended big-league games that year. The average per-game crowd was 32,785 fans. Minor League Baseball set an attendance record in 2007, too. More than 42,800,000 fans watched minor-league games that year. The 30 big-league teams averaged about 2.65 million fans each in '07. Eight teams set single-season franchise records, including the Yankees, who established an American League mark with more than 4.2 million fans. (Historical note: In 1920, the Yankees were the first team ever to draw more than 1 million fans over the course of a season.) The Major League record is held by the Colorado Rockies, who attracted 4.48 million fans in their inaugural season in 1993.

In March of 2008, an exhibition game between the Boston Red Sox and the Los Angeles Dodgers drew the largest crowd in baseball history. Some 115,300 crammed the Los Angeles Memorial Coliseum as part of the Dodgers' 50th anniversary celebration. The team had played regularly in the Coliseum during its first four years in Los Angeles from 1958 to 1961. In 1959, the Dodgers hosted the largest World Series crowd ever: 92,706 for a game against the Chicago White Sox.

Before 2008, the largest crowd to see a baseball game was 114,000. That came in Melbourne, Australia, during the 1956 Olympics. That day, the Australian National Team played an exhibition against an American services team.

■ *These fans at a 2007 Cardinals' game helped baseball set another attendance record.*

Bagwell, Jeff

A feared slugger during the 1990s, Bagwell played his entire 15-year career with the Houston Astros. After winning the 1992 Rookie of the Year award and the 1994 MVP crown, Bagwell continued as one of baseball's best hitters for a decade. He hit above .300 six times, was a four-time All-Star, and led the National League in runs three times. Famous for his extremely wide batting stance, Bagwell was primarily a first baseman. He made his only World Series appearance in 2005, when the Astros were swept by the White Sox. Bagwell retired after the 2006 season.

Baker, Frank

Few players in baseball history deserved their nicknames less than Frank "Home Run" Baker. A solid third baseman for the Philadelphia Athletics from 1908 to 1922, Baker earned his famous new name thanks to hitting only a pair of homers during the 1911 World Series, which the A's ended up winning. Baker never had more than 12 homers in a season, but the nickname stuck. However, in his defense, that was a pretty big total in those days. "Home Run" Baker landed in the Hall of Fame in 1955.

Balk

A balk (rhymes with "walk") is called by an umpire when a pitcher starts to make his delivery, then stops for any reason. A balk can also be called for other illegal movements by a pitcher. This allows each baserunner to move up one base. A balk cannot be called with nobody on base. The reason for the balk rule is to prevent pitchers from "pretending" to pitch and catching baserunners off base.

Ball

A pitch that does not cross the strike zone and is not swung at by the batter is called a "ball" by the umpire. If a batter gets four balls during an at-bat before he gets three strikes, he gets a "base on balls," also known as a "walk."

Ballparks

The places where baseball is played. Ballparks started as little more than open fields where players would mark out a diamond. Through use, the basepaths were more firmly set, and the empty field became home to regular games. The first place that was enclosed and used to hold baseball games was in Brooklyn, New York, in 1862. By the early days of pro baseball in the 1870s, most large cities boasted enclosed structures with seating for fans and dugouts for players to sit in. The outfield was enclosed by a wall or fence of some sort. In some cities, the ballparks simply fit into an existing park and could often have unusual shapes. Fenway Park in Boston is a good example. Because a street ran behind one edge of the ballpark site, a large wall was built to shelter the street, allowing only about 300 feet to home plate, which is shorter than usual. Other parks, such as the Polo Grounds in New York City, had unusual shapes. Its enormous oval design created very short corners of the outfield and a huge, deep center field.

Today, ballparks are created to blend the best of the style of old-time places with all the modern additions available, from high-tech scoreboards to luxury suites with every food imaginable. For true fans, however, the outfield bleachers are still the best place to sit. See the Appendix (page 84) for a complete list of ballparks used today in Major League Baseball.

■ *Banks was a two-time MVP for his beloved Cubs.*

Baltimore Orioles

Please see pages 24–25.

Banks, Ernie

 The man known as "Mr. Cub" was much loved both during and after his Hall-of-Fame career. Banks kept his sunny personality shining for 19 years with the Cubs, though he never tasted any postseason success. Banks is also the only player to win back-to-back MVP awards while on a last place team (1958–59).

Banks grew up in Texas and became a star, first in semipro leagues and then in the Negro Leagues with the Kansas City Monarchs. After a stint in the Army, he signed with the Chicago Cubs and joined the Major League team in 1953. By the late 1950s, he was among baseball's best players. He was also its best-hitting shortstop. Few players at that position boasted power; Banks would end his career with 512 homers.

By 1962, though, problems with his knees forced a move to the less-athletic

continued on page 26

23

■ *Brooks Robinson celebrates at the '66 World Series.*

Baltimore Orioles

When speaking of the Baltimore Orioles, make sure to separate the old ones from the new ones. The Baltimore Orioles of the 1890s were one of the great teams of its time, featuring many Hall of Fame players. However, they turned into the New York Highlanders—and later the Yankees.

The Baltimore Orioles of today have their roots in another city. From 1901 until 1954, the St. Louis Browns were one of baseball's least-successful teams. They regularly finished at or near the bottom of the standings and they included only a few star players. Perhaps the best was Hall-of-Fame first baseman George Sisler, who batted .420 in 1922 and once held the single-season record of 257 hits. The Browns won only one A.L. pennant, in 1944, and then lost in the World Series to their crosstown rivals, the St. Louis Cardinals.

In 1954, the team was sold and moved to Baltimore, where it took the nickname of those long-ago famous Orioles. The team had some success in the early 1960s, but really took off later in the decade. The Orioles built a very strong pitching staff, and featured sluggers such as first baseman Boog Powell and outfielder Frank Robinson, who won the Triple Crown in 1966. At third base, Brooks Robinson was setting a new standard for defense on the "hot corner."

In 1966, the slugging of the Robinsons and the pitching of young Jim Palmer led the O's to their greatest success, as they won their first A.L. pennant and then beat the Dodgers in the World Series.

In 1969, manager Earl Weaver led the Orioles to the first of their six A.L. East Division titles. The team led the A.L. in ERA for five seasons starting in 1969. Baltimore lost the World Series in 1969 to the Mets, but came back to win it all again in 1970.

That year, the Orioles became the first team with four 20-game winners: Mike Cuellar, Dave McNally, Pat Dobson, and Palmer. In the World Series, Brooks Robinson became an all-time hero with a series of amazing defensive plays, and the Orioles beat the Reds.

Baltimore returned to the World Series in 1971 and 1979, but lost both times. However, a new crop of young players, led by shortstop Cal Ripken Jr., carried Baltimore back to the top in 1983. The Orioles beat the Phillies to win another Series title.

Unfortunately, though Ripken was continuing a games-played streak that would make him a legend, the Orioles fell on hard times. In 1988, they lost their first 21 games of the season, a record that no team wants to hold.

The biggest news in the next decade was the opening, in 1992, of Oriole Park at Camden Yards, a fabulous new ballpark. The brick-covered stadium was the first of many new ballparks that recalled classic old designs but also featured lots of modern touches.

Three years later, the stadium was the site of one of the biggest moments in baseball history. Ripken

■ *The numbers show Ripken's new record.*

played in his 2,131st straight game, beating the amazing record of the great Lou Gehrig. He was saluted by the fans with a 20-minute ovation. The event helped baseball recover from a players' strike the year before.

The Orioles made the playoffs in 1996 and 1997, and Ripken reached 3,000 hits. His streak finally ended in 1998 at 2,632 games. Unfortunately, that's just about the only thrilling thing for Baltimore fans in the past decade, as they have not been very successful in a competitive A.L. East.

BALTIMORE ORIOLES

LEAGUE: **AMERICAN**

DIVISION: **EAST**

YEAR FOUNDED: **1901**

CURRENT COLORS: **ORANGE AND BLACK**

STADIUM (CAPACITY): **ORIOLE PARK AT CAMDEN YARDS (48,262)**

ALL-TIME RECORD (THROUGH 2008): **7,949–8,765**

WORLD SERIES TITLES (MOST RECENT): **3 (1983)**

■ *To keep them in place, bases fit into holes in the field.*

position of first base. By the late 1960s, his inability to run well caused problems with his game and with his manager, Leo Durocher. Some felt that Banks might have stayed in a game a bit too long. But no one wanted him to leave, either; few men in the game have ever been as universally beloved as Banks. His enthusiasm for the game he loved was well known. One of his most famous sayings was, "It's a great day for a ball game; let's play two!"

Banks retired in 1971 and was elected to the Hall of Fame in 1977. He remains a great ambassador for his Cubs and for baseball.

Barber, Red

Walter "Red" Barber was perhaps the most famous and influential baseball radio broadcaster ever. He started out with the Cincinnati Reds in 1934, and moved to the Brooklyn Dodgers in 1938. With the Dodgers, he gained national fame for his easy-going, friendly style. "The Old Redhead" brought the details of every game home to Brooklyn fans, but he did it in the voice of the old South (Barber grew up in Mississippi). His famous expressions included "Oh, doctor!" and "They're tearin' up the pea patch!" In 1939, he became the first baseball announcer on TV; he did the first televised World Series in 1948.

In 1954, Barber moved over to the New York Yankees. During that team's great World Series run of the 1950s and 1960s, he teamed with fellow radio legend Mel Allen to bring the games to New York fans. He was fired by the Yankees in 1966, to the dismay of many.

In 1978, in honor of his many accomplishments, Barber (along with Mel Allen) was given the first Ford Frick Award by the Hall of Fame. The honor now goes every year to a longtime broadcaster who deserves a place among baseball's best.

Base

Located 90 feet (27 m) apart, three bases and home plate form the square, or diamond, that is the heart of a baseball field. First, second, and third bases must be reached by a batter-turned-baserunner in order to then touch home and score a run for his team. The bases themselves are usually a thick pad covered by heavy plastic. They are anchored to the ground by a short post. In early baseball, the bases were stuffed leather sacks, leading to the still-used slang term of "bags" for bases.

Baseball

A baseball is a sphere about 9 inches (23 cm) around that weighs between 5 and 5.25 ounces (142–149 g). It is covered by two pieces of leather shaped like the number "8." These two pieces interlock and are held together by stitched thread. The inside of today's baseball contains a central "pill" of leather and rubber, surrounded by hundreds of yards of wound cotton and wool thread or string.

Baseballs have generally been the same size since the game's early days, but the interior parts and the outer casing have changed over the years. Also, because they were expensive and hard to make, early baseballs were often used for much longer periods. In early games, one ball might last a whole game, starting out nice and hard and ending up a soggy mess. Pitchers could also, until 1920, smear the outside of the ball with spit, tar, grease, or other substances to make it move in odd ways.

In today's Major Leagues, a typical ball lasts only six pitches before being taken out of play one way or another. Younger players might use a softer, rubber-covered ball to help them learn to play.

Baseball Cards

These colorful rectangles of cardboard include photos of players and information about their careers. The cards are created by companies for fans, who collect huge sets of them or just pick those of their favorite players. Baseball cards began as advertisements for tobacco or gum in the 1860s. Until the 1980s, most packs of cards were sold to children and included a stick of gum or perhaps stickers. In the 1980s, however, an explosion of interest in cards—especially the value of older, historic

■ *Five dozen baseballs are needed for one Major League game.*

Baseball, History of

Although baseball is known as "America's National Pastime," exactly how the sport actually began is a subject covered in mystery.

People have been playing games with sticks and balls for centuries. Ancient Egyptian paintings show people swinging a stick at what looks like a ball. However, baseball's roots seem to come mostly from games played in England in the 1600s and 1700s, especially one that is still played today called "rounders."

The most-told story about how baseball began regards a game in 1845 as the "first" baseball game. It was played in Hoboken, New Jersey, between two New York City sports clubs: the Knickerbocker Club, which organized the game and wrote down some rules for the game for the first time, and the New York Club. The latter team won 23-1.

However, in recent decades, historians have uncovered several earlier references to a game called "baseball" or "base ball," as it was written back then. Historian John Thorn found a 1791 law in Massachusetts that banned baseball from being played near the town's church; it was feared that a ball might break a window! In 2008, a reference in an English diary from 1755 mentions the author playing "baseball" with some friends. And a 1734 book for children includes the term "base ball" in a short poem.

Another problem with tracking down the origins of baseball is what is known as the "Doubleday Myth." In 1907, Albert Spalding, a former big-league pitcher turned sporting-goods bigshot, organized a committee to discover once and for all how baseball began. However, he didn't want the answer to be that the game evolved from earlier, British games. He wanted America's "national game" to be American-born. He got what he wanted in the form of a letter from a man named Abner Graves, saying he had been in Cooperstown, New York, when Abner Doubleday, later a Union Army general, set up the first baseball diamond.

Spalding then put out this story as fact and the town of Cooperstown got a name as the "birthplace of baseball."

One problem: Doubleday had never been to Cooperstown and he never mentioned baseball during his lifetime. The story was completely false. But because Spalding was a good salesman, you'll still find books today, more than 100 years later, that credit Gen. Doubleday as inventing baseball. Don't believe them!

Who should get credit? Most historians today thank Alexander Cartwright and other members of the Knickerbocker Club with organizing what had been several different

■ *This 1863 painting shows a baseball game being played at a Civil War prison camp.*

stick-and-ball game into one. They were the first to put a set distance between bases—they used "30 paces," now equal to 90 feet (27 m)—and the first to set the number of players and innings. The rules have evolved over the years, of course, but the "Knickerbocker Game" is as close as we'll ever come to knowing how baseball began.

We do know for sure, however, that once some basic rules were established, the game grew quickly in popularity. The Civil War (1861–65) played a big part in spreading the game, as soldiers from both sides traveled the country and brought their game with them, showing it to more people along the way. There's a famous painting of a baseball game being played at a Confederate prison camp in 1863.

The first teams were made up of amateur players and members of sports clubs. Professional teams began in 1869; the Cincinnati Red Stockings were the first. The first league of teams was formed in 1871. By 1876, the National League was playing. In 1901, the American League joined it, and the "Major Leagues" were born.

Since those days in the mid-19th century, baseball has boomed. Until the 1960s, it was far and away America's favorite sport. In recent years, pro football has passed baseball in terms of what is the fan favorite. However, in the past two seasons, more people have attended Major League Baseball games than ever. Because of its long history and connection with Americans, baseball remains "America's National Pastime."

ADRIAN C. ANSON.
ALLEN & GINTER'S
RICHMOND. *Cigarettes.* VIRGINIA

■ *An example of an early baseball card from a tobacco company.*

cards—led to millions more cards being made and sold. The enthusiasm for cards has died back down since then, but they remain a (gum-free) part of most fans' enjoyment of baseball.

The 1980s boom in cards led to very high prices for the rarest cards. A rare Honus Wagner card from 1909 has sold for as much as $2.8 million, while a Mickey Mantle rookie card from 1951 has reached $160,000.

Baseball Hall of Fame

Located in Cooperstown, New York, the Hall of Fame honors the greatest people in the game's history. It also displays hundreds of exhibits of baseball gear from more than 150 years of history. Thousands more pieces of memorabilia not on display are kept by the Hall for research and future exhibits. The Hall also has a library and an enormous photo collection.

Each year, the Baseball Writers Association of America elects new members of the Hall of Fame. On a weekend in July or August, the new members are introduced to a crowd of thousands and a national TV audience. The writers can elect players, managers, umpires, owners, or executives,.

The Hall also honors writers and broadcasters in special elections.

Why Cooperstown? In 1909, a report said baseball was "invented" there in 1839. Nothing could be further from the truth, but the mistake stuck. In 1939, the Hall of Fame was opened in this upstate New York village, thanks to a mistake!

Baseball, History of

Please see pages 28–29.

Base Coaches

Stationed in foul ground near first and third bases, these coaches help base runners. They relay signals from the managers and make sure baserunners know the game situation. They also tell players who have just hit the ball whether to keep running to the next base or to stop. Beginning in 2008, base coaches were required to wear plastic helmets for safety.

Baseline

The baseline is the space between two bases. The lines between first and second and second and third are usually not marked on the field, while the lines from home to first and third to home are lined with chalk or paint. These latter two lines are also called foul lines, because they show the separation between foul and fair territory (the line itself is in fair territory). A baserunner can be called out for going

■ *When a ball is hit, baserunners sprint toward the next base, trying to reach it before being tagged.*

out of the baseline to avoid being tagged, although they do not have to run along the exact baseline.

Baserunner

Any player who is on base safely becomes a baserunner. He can advance to his next base when his teammates put the ball in play, on a wild pitch or passed ball, or by stealing a base.

Bases Loaded

A situation in which there is a baserunner on each of first, second, and third bases. Some of the fun slang terms for this excellent offensive situation include "bags full" or "ducks on the pond."

Bat

A rounded wood stick used to hit a pitched baseball. Bats at the professional level have always been made of wood, from ash to hickory to maple. Bats at just about every other level are usually made of aluminum, a switch that took place starting in the 1970s. Wood bats break, of course, and have to be replaced, while aluminum bats can last much longer. Debate continues among youth leagues whether to go back to wood. It is seen as safer than aluminum, which can put a bit more power into hits.

Bats are made on a lathe, a machine that turns rapidly while another machine or a craftsperson carves the bat into its

■ *Bats labeled with players' uniform numbers.*

shape. Pro players are very particular about their bats, and make sure that they always get the right weight and length. Pro bats usually weigh from about 31 to 38 ounces (878–1077 g) and are 33 to 38 inches (84–97 cm) long. Bats at youth levels vary according to the age and size of the kids.

Batboy

A person (often a teenager) who works with players and umpires during games. The duties of a batboy (or batgirl) include retrieving bats and baseballs, bring-ing new baseballs to the umpires, cleaning the dugout, and helping players with what-ever gear they might need. Many batboys also work in the clubhouse before and after games helping with team laundry, cleanup, and other duties.

Batter's Box

The rectangular areas on either side of home plate where a batter must stand during a pitch. Though the chalk lines that define the box often disappear during a game, a batter must still remain in those areas. If he hits a pitch while stepping out of the batter's box, the umpire can call him out.

Batting Average

A statistic that shows how often a player gets a base hit. To figure batting average (often abbreviated BA), divide the total number of base hits by the number of official at-bats. A hitter with an average of above .300 (or 3 hits out of every 10 at-bats) is regarded as a good hitter.

Batting Glove

A glove made of thin nylon or leather worn by a batter to improve his grip on the bat. Batters who use just one glove wear it on their bottom hand; that is, the hand closest to the knob of the bat. Some players choose to wear a batting glove on each hand, however.

Batting Helmet

A hard-plastic head covering worn by batters and baserunners. Helmets protect players when they are hit by pitches or thrown balls. Batting helmets were not mandatory in the Majors until 1956, and even then were little more than pieces of plastic worn inside the cap. By 1971, all players had to wear a full, padded, hard-plastic helmet. Today's helmets have an earflap on the side facing the pitcher. Many youth leagues provide helmets with face guards as well.

Batting Practice

Before a game, players hit easy pitches thrown by a coach to get their swings warmed up. Players usually stand inside an open-fronted cage or netting to keep balls from being hit into the stands. Players who are great at batting practice but don't do well in games are called "five o'clock hitters," as that is about when many home teams hold BP, as it is known.

Bell, "Cool Papa"

When reading about super-speedy Negro League outfielder James "Cool Papa" Bell, it's hard to tell where the facts stop and the legends begin. The great pitcher Satchel Paige once said that Bell was so fast, he hit a line drive that hit Bell as he rounded second. Another story said he could flip a light switch and be in bed before the room got dark. Those are stories, of course, but they were based on his truly remarkable speed. In 1933, he was timed running around all four bases in 12 seconds. The fastest major leaguer to that point had done it in 13.3 seconds. Bell, however, never got the chance to truly test his speed and batting skills (it was estimated that he had a .340-plus lifetime average) against Major Leaguers. Instead, he played in the Negro Leagues from 1922 to 1946.

But Major Leaguers saw him play and knew that he'd have been among the best in their league, too. Famed owner Bill

■ *For right-handers, the helmet earflap is on the left.*

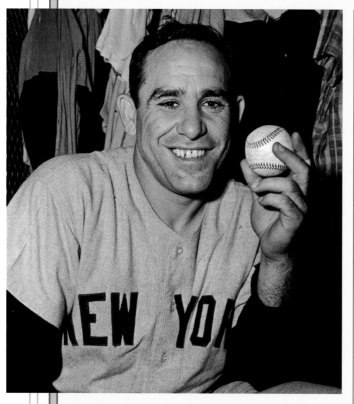

■ *Yogi was a regular in the World Series.*

Berra, Yogi

One of baseball's most beloved figures, Berra was also one of its most successful. Thanks to helping the Yankees win 10 World Series in his 19 years with the team, Berra holds many career World Series batting marks. He is the all-time leader in World Series games, at-bats, and hits, and is second in runs and RBI. Berra also has 10 World Series rings, the most ever. For all that, and even with three A.L. MVP awards, Berra is perhaps best known for his strange ability to say, well . . . strange things (see box).

Lawrence Peter Berra got his nickname as a kid after his friends saw an Indian actor in a movie that reminded them of Berra, and Lawrence became "Yogi" (a Hindu word for teacher). After growing up in St. Louis and serving in the Navy during World War II, then spending several years in the minors, Berra joined the Yankees in 1949. He was a backup that year and a starter the next, and the Yankees won the World Series both years, the first pair of a record five in a row. Berra's solid bat and great catching played a big part in the team's success. In a league that boasted stars such as Mickey Mantle, Al Kaline, and Ted Williams, Berra won A.L. MVP awards in 1951, 1954, and 1955.

By the early 1960s, Berra had moved to the outfield to save his legs. From there, he

THE SAYINGS OF YOGI

"It ain't over 'til it's over."

"When you come to a fork in the road . . . take it!"

"It gets late out early here."

"You can observe a lot by watching."

"Ninety percent of the game is half mental."

"If the world were perfect, it wouldn't be."

"I didn't really say everything I said."

■ *Berra was later a Yankees' manager.*

helped the Yanks win two more Series (1961 and 1962). After 1963, Berra left the field and became the Yankees' manager; the team won the 1964 A.L. pennant. He later also coached the Mets to a spot in the World Series. He returned to manage the Yankees briefly in 1984, but was fired after 22 games by owner George Steinbrenner. Berra was so hurt that he didn't return to Yankee Stadium for 15 years. Today, Berra spends most of his time working at the Yogi Berra Museum in New Jersey. He was elected to the Hall of Fame in 1972 and was chosen to baseball's All-Century Team for the 1900s.

Veeck once called Bell, "the equal of Joe DiMaggio or Willie Mays." During exhibition games against white players, Bell batted .378.

Though his career was over by the time the unfair "color barrier" fell in 1947 (see Jackie Robinson and Integration of Baseball), Bell was thrilled when his fellow African-Americans finally got their chance. And for his many accomplishments, he was elected to the Hall of Fame in 1974. Getting there was about the only thing Cool Papa didn't do fast.

Beltran, Carlos

The Puerto Rico-born outfielder combines power and speed like few players in baseball. Beltran was the 1999 Rookie of the Year with Kansas City. That season, he had more than 20 steals and 20 homers for the first of seven times in his career. In fact, he topped 30 steals four times. In the middle of the 2004 season, he was traded to Houston. Between those two teams, he joined the 30–30 Club, with 30 steals and homers in the same season. Beltran signed a big free-agent contract with the Mets to start the 2005 season.

With New York, Beltran has been a four-time All-Star and won a pair of Gold Gloves. Beltran has a total of seven seasons with 100 or more RBI. He remains a feared slugger and a talented all-around star.

■ *Bench played his entire career in Cincinnati.*

Bench, Johnny

In the discussion of greatest catchers of all time, Johnny Bench has a permanent place. Few catchers combined defensive excellence with batting skill like Bench, who not only knocked in hundreds of runs, but also changed the way many catchers approach their position.

Bench grew up in Oklahoma. A hitting star from an early age, he earned the nickname the "Binger Banger" after his hometown. By 1968, he was the N.L. Rookie of the Year with the Cincinnati Reds and had earned the first of 13 straight All-Star Game selections. Bench struggled a bit defensively in his early seasons, but by consistently using only one hand to catch, he changed the way catchers played. Before then, most catchers brought their throwing hand out to cover up the ball in the mitt after catching it. Bench's style was easier for him because of his very powerful throwing arm. He wanted the ball in his hand right away to throw out potential base-stealers. He would eventually earn 10 Gold Gloves for fielding excellence.

By 1970, Bench was the N.L. MVP after leading the league with 45 homers and 145 RBI. The Reds made it to the World Series, but lost to Baltimore. Two years later, he was the MVP again, with 40 more dingers and 125 RBI. He helped the Reds win the World Series in 1975 and 1976; he was the MVP of the '76 Series. Toward the end of his career, Bench played first base, third base, and outfield, but it was his years as a catcher that sent him, in 1989, to join the heroes in the Baseball Hall of Fame. Ten years later, when baseball chose the All-Century Team for the 1900s, Bench was only one of two catchers chosen (the other catcher was Yogi Berra).

Berra, Yogi

Please see page 34.

Biggio, Craig

In a busy 20-year career with the Houston Astros, Craig Biggio set himself apart for many reasons. After becoming a base-stealing All-Star catcher by 1991 (most catchers don't steal bases), he moved to second base and made the All-Star team there, too, later winning four Gold Gloves at his new position. Though not blessed with home-run power, Biggio led the league in doubles four times. He also had great speed, stealing 30 or more bases five times.

His most unique success, however, came at a price. Biggio was hit by pitches 285 times in his career, an all-time high. Also, in 1998, Biggio topped 50 steals and 50 doubles in the same season, only the second time that had ever been done. Biggio was one of the most skilled and dependable players in baseball for the 1990s and early 2000s. He reached 3,000 hits in 2007 and retired after the season.

Big Red Machine

A nickname for the Cincinnati Reds, primarily the World Series-winning teams of 1975 and 1976.

"Black Sox"

This is the nickname given to the 1919 Chicago White Sox. Several months after this mighty team was upset by the Cincinnati Reds in the World Series, it was revealed that some of the players on the team were paid money by gamblers to "throw" games, or lose on purpose. This was against the law and against the rules of baseball. Eventually, eight players, including legendary hitter "Shoeless Joe" Jackson, were charged with a crime. A jury found them not guilty. They were not as lucky with baseball, however. The new commissioner, Kenesaw Mountain Landis, banned all eight from ever playing again. The entire baseball world was stunned, first at the effect of gambling and second at the harsh penalty. Many fans were also hurt by the players' actions, saying that they could not be sure they believed that all the games were fair. The "stain" on baseball lasted for quite a while.

Landis' ban stood, although several of the players claimed that they had never really taken money. Star outfielder Jackson tried for many years to be allowed back in the game, but he never was. To this day, the man with the third-highest batting average of all time (.356) cannot be elected to the Hall of Fame because of Landis' ban.

Bleachers

The seating areas around the outfield of a ballpark. Bleachers usually do not have individual seats. Fans sit on benches instead. Early bleachers almost always were uncovered areas. They got their name for the way the hot afternoon sun would "bleach" the painted wood.

■ *Boggs ate chicken before every game.*

Boggs, Wade

One of the finest hitters of recent decades, Boggs won five A.L. batting titles in the 1980s and earned 12 straight All-Star selections. A third baseman, he hit better than .300 in five minor-league seasons. He finally made it to the Majors with Boston in 1982; his .349 average was the highest ever for an A.L. rookie. He quickly established himself as the man to beat in the batting race. A left-handed hitter, he could hit equally well to all fields, but with little power. He had five seasons

Bonds, Barry

Barry Bonds hit more home runs (762) and won more Most Valuable Player Awards (seven) than any other player in baseball history. Unfortunately, he has become more well-known for things away from the baseball field. He was at the center of the illegal steroids scandal of the early 2000s, and in 2007 was accused by the U.S. Government of lying under oath. While his case continues and many questions about him remain unanswered, one thing is clear: Barry Bonds was surely one of the most talented athletes in baseball history.

Bonds followed in the footsteps of his father Bobby, who was a speedy outfielder for 14 years, mostly for the San Francisco Giants. Barry was a star at Arizona State and joined the Pittsburgh Pirates in 1986. He quickly became one of baseball's best players. Bonds combined batting skill and speed on the bases like few players ever. In 1990, he won the first of his record-setting seven MVP awards. He finished second in the MVP voting in 1991 and then won again in '92 and '93.

Bonds signed a huge free-agent contract to join the Giants, his dad's old team, before the 1993 season. He started hitting more and more homers, as well as batting for a high average. Bonds had 46 homers in 1993, the first of eight seasons he would top 40. He also had 11 seasons with an average above .300. He kept stealing bases, too, recording five 30–30 seasons (30 homers and 30 steals) and one 40–40 year (1996). He also played great defense, winning eight Gold Gloves and a reputation as one of the best left fielders ever.

But he was just getting started. After the turn of the new century, Bonds went on a home-run tear like no had ever seen. In 2001, he amazed the baseball world by hitting 73, breaking the single-season mark of 70 put up only three years earlier by Mark McGwire. Bonds' career home run total, meanwhile, kept rising quickly, and many thought he had a chance to top Hank Aaron's record of 755.

However, a cloud emerged as Bonds approached the record. More and more players were being accused of using illegal steroids, drugs that helped them become stronger and, perhaps, hit more homers. The trainer who worked with Bonds was charged with crimes relating to these drugs. Bonds himself denied it all, but few believed him. Part of the reason was his attitude, which was not the fan-friendly, team-oriented approach that people expected from their heroes. Bonds seemed to act and feel like he was above other people, that he deserved special treatment.

Amid all this controversy, Bonds kept hitting homers, and finally, in 2007, he did it: He cracked his 756th homer on August 8 against the Washington Nationals. His hometown

■ *Bonds also set records for most walks.*

fans stood and cheered; few others in baseball joined them.

Bonds was charged with lying under oath following the 2007 season. He was not signed by any team to play in 2008. The case in court goes on. Only time will tell if Bonds becomes as liked off the field as he was successful on it.

■ *Lou Boudreau: a leader on and off the field.*

above .350 and seven seasons with 200 or more hits. He won his first batting title in 1983 and then won every year from 1985 to 1988. After slumping in the early 1990s, he moved to the Yankees and hit .300 in his first four years in New York. He also won his first World Series ring, helping the Yanks to the title in 1996. He famously rode a police horse around the Yankee Stadium outfield after the winning game. Boggs wound up his career in 1997 with his hometown Tampa Bay Devil Rays. With Tampa Bay, he reached 3,000 hits for his career—No. 3,000 came on a homer! Boggs was elected to the Hall of Fame in 2005.

Boston Braves

Please see pages 18–19, Atlanta Braves.

Boston Red Sox

Please see pages 42–43.

Boudreau, Lou

It's hard enough being a Hall-of-Fame-level shortstop—imagine having to be the team manager, too! That's the task that Lou Boudreau did for the Indians from 1942 to 1951. Boudreau got the job of player-manager after writing to the team owner. In a surprise move, the team made its 24-year-old star shortstop the youngest manager in league history. While running the ball club off the field, Boudreau led by example on it. He was the top-fielding shortstop in the league eight times, and he was the A.L. batting champ in 1944.

As a manager, Boudreau was always looking to try something new. He popularized a defense called the "Williams Shift," moving his entire team toward right field to counter the great left-handed batter Ted Williams. He turned former outfielder Bob Lemon into one of the best pitchers in the American League.

In 1948, Boudreau led the Indians into a one-game playoff for the A.L. pennant against Williams and the Red Sox. Again, Lou led the way, with a pair of homers in the 8–3 win. The Indians went on to win the World Series against the Braves.

■ *Fans seated in box seats might pay a little more for their tickets, but they get a chance to catch foul balls.*

Boudreau played for the Red Sox and Athletics and also managed the Cubs. He became a popular radio broadcaster. Boudreau made the Hall of Fame in 1970.

Box Score

A handy way to record all the results of a single game. This statistical chart includes the lineups of the teams, what each batter did (at-bats, runs, hits, and RBI), and what each pitcher did (innings pitched and strikeouts, and walks, runs, and hits allowed). Other information might include a "line score" that shows which team scored in which innings, who had extra-base hits, who the umpires were, how long the game took to play, and even the attendance. The box score is a great way to get a summary of an entire game. Writer Henry Chadwick is credited with making the box score popular. He was inspired by a scoring system used in the British game of cricket.

Box Seats

Often the best and most expensive seats at most ballparks, these are located closest to the field along the first

continued on page 45

Boston Red Sox

Young fans of the Boston Red Sox might think that their team has always been as great as they have been in recent years, with two World Series titles since 2004. But longtime fans know that for most of the 20th century, the Red Sox broke their fans' hearts time and again. Often among the best teams in baseball, the Red Sox couldn't break through to win it all, going from 1918 until 2004 without a World Series title.

It wasn't always that way. In fact, in the early 1900s, the Red Sox won five World Series before 1919.

The Red Sox first played in 1901, the first year of the American League. They were the champions of the new league by 1903, helped by superstar pitcher Cy Young. After that season, the team (then known as the Americans) played in the first World Series. They beat the N.L.-champion Pittsburgh Pirates and became the first official World Champions. Boston won the A.L. pennant again in 1904, but the New York Giants refused to play them in the World Series. By 1912, the team had added starting pitcher "Smoky" Joe Wood and great outfielders Tris Speaker and Harry Hooper. That year, a lovely new ballpark opened in Boston, in a part of town called the Fens. Fenway Park is still the home of the Red Sox and is the oldest ballpark still in use in the Majors.

Boston brought a World Series title to Fenway in its first season. Then in 1915, the Red Sox added a young left-handed pitcher named George Ruth (yes . . . Babe Ruth). They won their third World Series that season and repeated the feat in 1916. They added a fifth title in 1918, as Ruth combined his pitching skills with growing batting talent.

However, following the 1919 season, disaster struck the Red Sox. Owner Harry Frazee, looking for money to

■ *Carl Yastrzemski played for Boston for a record 23 seasons.*

finance a Broadway show, sold Ruth to the Yankees. The Red Sox didn't win again until 2004, causing many people to call the team's lack of luck the "Curse of the Bambino" (Bambino was another of Ruth's nicknames).

Tom Yawkey bought the Red Sox in 1933. In 1939, they added their greatest star, slugger Ted Williams, "the greatest hitter who ever lived." In 1941, he became the last player to top .400, at .406. However, even with Williams' talent, the Red Sox won only one pennant with him on the team, in 1946, and they lost that World Series in seven games.

That started a pattern. In 1967, 1975, and 1986, the Sox also won A.L. pennants, but lost Game Sevens in the World Series. Each time, they made it tough on their fans. In 1967, they pulled off the "Impossible Dream," beating out two other teams on the last day of the season to win the pennant. Carl "Yaz" Yastrzemski, who took over for Williams as the star left fielder for Boston, won the Triple Crown (a league title in homers, RBI, and batting average). In 1975, Boston won Game Six of the World Series, as Carlton Fisk hit one of baseball's most famous homers, winning the

game in the 12th inning. In 1986, the Red Sox were one strike away from beating the Mets in Game Six, but Boston gave the game away. They lost the Series the next night.

Finally, in 2004, years of frustration for "Red Sox Nation" ended. Trailing the Yankees three games to none in the ALCS, and down to their last out in the ninth inning of Game Four, the Red Sox rallied. They won that night, then won three more over

■ *Catcher and captain Jason Varitek.*

the Yanks, then swept the Cardinals in the World Series. All of Boston, all of New England, and Red Sox fans across America cried as the Curse of the Bambino was finally lifted. Three years later, in 2007, still led by sluggers Manny Ramirez and David Ortiz, catcher and captain Jason Varitek, and joined by relief ace Jonathan Papelbon, Boston did it again. The Red Sox swept Colorado to win another title.

BOSTON RED SOX

LEAGUE: **AMERICAN**

DIVISION: **EAST**

YEAR FOUNDED: **1901**

CURRENT COLORS:
RED, BLUE, AND WHITE

STADIUM (CAPACITY):
**FENWAY PARK
(36,108)**

ALL-TIME RECORD
(THROUGH 2008):
8,635–8,093

WORLD SERIES TITLES
(MOST RECENT):
7 (2007)

Brett, George

Of all the great hitters in baseball history, only George Brett won a batting title in three different decades. By 1975, his second year with the Royals, Brett was hitting above .300; he would top that mark 11 times in his career. In 1976, he was the A.L. batting champion. His all-around great play was vital to Kansas City earning its first division title. Brett carried the Royals to the ALCS in 1978 and 1979, too. In 1980, he was even better.

■ *Brett watches one of his 3,154 hits.*

One of the rarest hitting feats is topping a .400 average for a season, and Brett came as close as anyone in the past 50 years, finishing at .390. He was the A.L. MVP and led the Royals to their first World Series appearance. They lost to Philadelphia, but Brett hit .375.

In 1983, Brett made news for another reason. In a game against the Yankees, his two-run homer gave the Royals the lead. But New York manager Billy Martin asked the umpires to check Brett's bat. They ruled that the bat had too much pine tar on it. Pine tar helps players get a better grip on the bat. The umps called Brett out and took away the homer. (It later was restored.) A famous TV clip shows Brett, red-faced and screaming, charging out of the dugout to protest.

In 1985, Brett had a career-high 30 homers and a league-best .585 slugging percentage. Brett and the Royals won the pennant again and this time finally won the World Series, too. In the "I-85 Series," named for the highway that connects Kansas City and St. Louis, the Royals beat the Cardinals in seven games. Brett now had a World Series ring to go with his batting titles.

He added a third batting title in 1990, somewhat of a surprise so late in his career. By this time, he had also moved to first base and DH. Brett got his 3,000th hit in 1992 and finished with 3,154. In 1999, he was elected to the Hall of Fame.

and third base lines. The name came from the fact that in early stadiums, these special seating areas were separated by low walls, forming actual boxes.

Boys of Summer

A nickname for the Brooklyn Dodgers of the 1950s. The author Roger Kahn wrote a very popular book by that name that told the story of those teams. The term can also be used to describe any group of baseball players.

Breaking Ball

A general term for any pitch that curves or changes direction, or any pitch other than a fastball or changeup. Breaking balls include curveballs, sliders, knuckleballs, and screwballs.

Bresnahan, Roger

The first catcher elected to the Hall of Fame (1945), Roger Bresnahan was also a catching pioneer. At the time he became a regular catcher in 1905, after playing outfield and infield for the Orioles and Giants, catchers didn't wear shin guards. In 1907, tired of foul balls whacking his legs, Bresnahan put on a pair of leg pads from the game of cricket. Though opponents made fun of him for being afraid, by the following year shin guards were in use throughout baseball. He was also a fine player, of course, and helped the Giants win the World Series in 1905. He later played for the Cardinals and Cubs before retiring in 1915.

Brock, Lou

Cardinals fans can always thank Bing Devine for giving them one of baseball's best basestealers. Devine traded fading pitcher Ernie Broglio to the Cubs in 1964 for an outfielder named Lou Brock, who was not expected to be a star. Always fast, Brock was not considered a great hitter. But that changed in St. Louis. He helped the Cards win the World Series in his first season with them. By 1967, he was leading the league in stolen bases (he won seven N.L. titles in that category) and also hitting around .300 regularly. His speed

■ *Stealing star Lou Brock slides in safely.*

This card shows famed pitcher Three-Finger Brown.

drove opponents crazy and he (along with the Dodgers' Maury Wills) helped make the stolen base a bigger part of baseball offense again. The Cardinals won another Series title in 1967 and the N.L. pennant in 1968.

In 1974, Brock's 118 stolen bases set a new single-season mark (breaking Wills' total of 104 from 1962). Three years later, Brock became the Majors' all-time leader, topping the great Ty Cobb's mark of 938 steals. Brock also topped 3,000 hits in 1979; the free swinger that Brock had been in his younger years had matured into one of big-league baseball's best batters.

Brock's single-season and career records have since fallen, but his impact on the game remains. He was elected to the Hall of Fame in 1985.

Bronx Bombers

A nickname for the New York Yankees. Yankee Stadium is located in a borough, or part, of New York City called The Bronx. The Yankees often boasted great home-run hitters, which helped create the nickname.

Brooklyn Dodgers

Please see Los Angeles Dodgers.

Brown, Mordecai "Three-Finger"

Even if Mordecai Peter Centennial Brown didn't have one of baseball's best nicknames–"Three-Finger"–he would still be well remembered for his pitching skills. His career ERA of 2.06 is third-lowest all-time, he won 20 games six times, and his 1.04 ERA in 1906 was the second-lowest of the 20th century. He helped the Cubs win the 1907 and 1908 World Series. (He also won the famous 1908 playoff game that gave Chicago the N.L. pennant.) But he did all this while pitching with a seriously injured right hand. A pair of farming accidents cost him his index finger and part of another, and left the remaining fingers oddly bent. But the injury gave his pitches unusual spin, and his bulldog personality let him fight through any problems. Brown retired in 1916 and was elected to the Hall of Fame in 1949.

Brushback Pitch

A pitch thrown at or near a batter that makes him lean back away from the plate to avoid being hit by the pitch. The pitcher is trying to "brush back" the hitter to keep the hitter from crowding the plate and having a better chance to get a hit. Brushback pitches that get too close can, of course, sometimes anger batters.

Bullpen

The area of a ballpark where relief pitchers warm up during a game and where a starting pitcher warms up before a game. Bullpens can be located behind outfield fences or along the outfield baselines. The word is also used to describe a group of a team's relief pitchers, as in, "The Red Sox have a great bullpen this season." The word probably comes from farming, as in a place to keep bulls or other animals.

Bunning, Jim

Jim Bunning holds a place in baseball history as one of 17 pitchers to throw a perfect game, which he did for the Phillies in 1964 against the New York Mets. He had long stints with the Phillies and, later, with the Detroit Tigers, and holds several marks for two-league pitchers. He is one of only a handful of pitchers with a no-hitter in each league; he held the Red Sox hitless in 1958 as a member of the Detroit Tigers. He was also the first pitcher to win more than 100 games, strike out 1,000 batters, and pitch in an All-Star Game in each league. Bunning retired in 1971 and later entered politics. He was a Congressman and U.S. Senator from Kentucky. Bunning entered the Hall of Fame in 1996.

Bunt

A play in which a batter deliberately hits the ball just a short way onto the field, usually by moving one hand up the barrel of the bat and tapping the pitch. Some bunts are made to try to reach base safely. Most bunts, however, are designed to be sacrifices—that is, the batter is trying to make himself be put out, a play that will allow a teammate to move up on the bases and into scoring position.

■ *This batter has "squared around" to bunt.*

■ *Cabrera is one of today's top young hitters.*

Cabrera, Miguel

It took only a few seasons for Miguel Cabrera to establish himself as one of the great young hitters in baseball today. He was just 24 when the Detroit Tigers signed the former Marlin to an eight-year contract worth more than $150 million in the spring of 2008.

Cabrera is a native of Venezuela who was signed by the Florida Marlins in 1999, when he was just 16 years old. By the middle of the 2003 season, he was in the Major Leagues. He drove in 62 runs in just 87 games that year and played a key role on the young Florida team that stunned the New York Yankees in seven games to win the 2003 World Series.

Cabrera made the All-Star Game in his first full season in '04, when he hit .294 with 33 home runs and 112 RBI. He followed that with three more All-Star seasons for the Marlins, driving in more than 110 runs each year and batting as high as .339 in 2006.

Although not a standout on defense, Cabrera played both third base and the outfield for the Marlins. The Tigers, after acquiring Cabrera via trade before the 2008 season, moved him to first base.

Cactus League

The Cactus League is not a typical league in which teams play a balanced schedule and a champion is crowned. Rather, it is a nickname for the big-league teams that hold their annual spring training camps in Arizona.

All Major League teams practice and train before the regular season in the warm climates of either Arizona or Florida. The teams that train in Florida play in the Grapefruit League.

Big-league teams have trained in Arizona since the Cleveland Indians and New York Giants began the tradition in 1946. In 2008, the 12 teams that played in the Cactus League included the Arizona Diamondbacks, Chicago Cubs, Chicago White Sox, Colorado Rockies, Kansas City

Royals, Los Angeles Angels of Anaheim, Milwaukee Brewers, Oakland Athletics, San Diego Padres, San Francisco Giants, Seattle Mariners, and Texas Rangers. The Los Angeles Dodgers were scheduled to leave their long-time spring home in Vero Beach, Florida, for a new site in Glendale, Arizona, in 2009.

California Angels

California Angels is the name under which the Los Angeles Angels of Anaheim (see Los Angeles Angels) played from 1965 through 1996.

The American League franchise began play as the Los Angeles Angels in 1961. Four years later, to forge an identity separate from the National League's Los Angeles Dodgers, the club changed its name to the California Angels. The next season, the franchise moved out of Los Angeles to Anaheim, California. In 1997, the team became known as the Anaheim Angels. In 2005, although the club remained in Anaheim, the team name changed again. This time, it officially became the Los Angeles Angels of Anaheim. However, the team is more commonly called simply the Los Angeles Angels.

■ *Players for the Angels wear practice jerseys as they warm up before a Cactus League game.*

Campanella, Roy

Few catchers in baseball history have been as good both offensively and defensively as Roy "Campy" Campanella, who starred for the Brooklyn Dodgers from 1948 to 1957. The three-time National League MVP was inducted into the Hall of Fame in 1969.

Before joining the Dodgers, Campanella was a star for seven seasons in the Negro Leagues–he was only 15 years old when

■ "Campy" was a three-time N.L. MVP.

he first played as a pro. One season after infielder Jackie Robinson broke Major League Baseball's color barrier, Campanella joined him in Brooklyn. In his third season, Campy belted 31 home runs and drove in 89 runs while batting .281. The next year, 1951, he earned the first of his MVP awards. His best season was 1953, when he batted .312 while setting big-league record records for a catcher with 42 home runs (one came as a pinch-hitter) and 142 RBI. His third MVP award came in 1955, when he helped the Dodgers win the World Series for the only time in Brooklyn.

Campanella's career ended after he was paralyzed in both arms and legs by injuries suffered in an automobile accident in January of 1958. The Dodgers moved to Los Angeles that year, but he remained with the club's community relations department until his death in 1993.

Canada, Baseball in

In 1969, Major League Baseball expanded beyond the borders of the United States for the first time in its history when the Montreal Expos joined the National League. Eight seasons later, the expansion Toronto Blue Jays joined the American League.

After struggling for the first decade of their existence, the Expos became a winning franchise noted for developing young stars, only to lose them to larger-market teams that were willing to pay them more. Montreal made the playoffs only once, falling to the Dodgers in the divisional round in 1981. The Expos' best team was in 1994, when they built baseball's best record (74–40) before the season was halted by a players' strike in August. The playoffs and World Series subsequently were canceled. After the 2004 season, the franchise relocated to Washington, D.C., and became known as the Nationals.

The Blue Jays are the only franchise from outside the United States to win a World Series. Toronto won back-to-back championships in 1992 and 1993, with the latter coming on Joe Carter's dramatic walk-off home run in the bottom of the ninth inning of the decisive Game Six against the Phillies.

While the Major Leagues did not place a team in Canada until 1969, the history of baseball in that country follows much the same time line as that of the United States. The first professional league, the International Association, began in 1877, just one year after the United States' National League was formed. The International Association featured teams from both Canada and the United States. Many Canadians have become stars in the Major Leagues, including All-Star Larry Walker, Hall-of-Fame pitcher Ferguson Jenkins, 2006 A.L. MVP Justin Morneau, and Red Sox outfielder Jason Bay.

■ *Cardinals star Albert Pujols models a cap.*

Cap

A cap, or baseball cap, is the hat worn by baseball players—but it's never called a hat!

Some form of headgear was worn in the field by baseball players as far back as the 1860s. But for many decades, the style varied widely from pillbox caps (which had flat tops) to floppy caps to short-billed caps. By the middle of the 20th century, the current baseball cap became standard: a rounded top with a longer bill to shade the eyes from the sun. Today's caps are made of wool or polyester, with a cloth-covered cardboard brim.

Caray, Harry

Harry Caray was a popular baseball play-by-play announcer for several Major League teams, although he is most associated with the Chicago Cubs. He is a member of the Radio Hall of Fame and has been honored in the broadcasters' wing of the Baseball Hall of Fame, receiving the Ford C. Frick Award.

Caray's long big-league career began with the Cardinals in 1945. He worked in St. Louis through 1969, then spent one season as the voice of the Oakland Athletics

■ *Hot-hitting Carew was an excellent fielder, too.*

before returning to the Midwest with the Chicago White Sox in 1971. In 1982, he shifted to Chicago's South Side and began working for the Cubs.

Caray reached the height of his popularity with the Cubs. Their games were telecast nationally on superstation WGN, and fans all around the country heard his famous calls, such as, "It might be . . . It could be . . . It is!" for Chicago home runs, and "Cubs win! Cubs win!" after each victory. He also led the crowd in singing "Take Me Out to the Ball-game" from the booth, and sometimes broadcast from the bleachers.

After his death at 83 in 1998, Harry was succeeded as the Cubs' announcer by Chip Caray, his grandson. Harry's son, Skip (Chip's dad), was a longtime broadcaster for the Atlanta Braves.

Carew, Rod

Rod Carew was one of the greatest pure hitters in big-league history. His bat control helped him amass 3,053 hits and put together a .328 batting average in a 19-year career from 1967 to 1985. In 1991, he was inducted into the Hall of Fame in his first year of eligibility.

A native of Panama, Carew made his Major League debut as a second baseman with the Minnesota Twins in 1967. Two years later, he hit .332

to begin a string of 15 seasons at .300 or better. He also won the first of his seven American League batting titles that year.

Carew, who used a variety of batting stances and styles, could stroke the ball to any field at any time. He could bunt well, too. After 12 productive seasons in Minnesota, he closed his career with seven years as a first baseman for the Angels.

In 1972, Carew hit .318 and became the first player to win the batting title without the benefit of a single home run. But, after sometimes being criticized as just a "singles hitter," he also posted a 14-homer, 100-RBI season for the Twins in 1977—the same season he hit an amazing .388 and was named the A.L. MVP.

Carew's great hitting overshadowed the fact that he was an excellent base runner, too. He stole 348 bases in his career, including a career-best 49 in 1976. In 1969, he equaled a still-existing Major League record by stealing home seven times.

Carlton, Steve

Hall-of-Famer Steve Carlton is considered one of the greatest left-handed pitchers in baseball history. In 24 big-league seasons from 1965 to 1988, he won 329 games. Warren Spahn (363 wins) is the only southpaw ever to win more.

Carlton's signature pitch was his slider, which he utilized along with his fastball to strike out 4,136 batters in his career. He

■ *Carlton excelled for less-than-great teams.*

was only the second player (after Nolan Ryan) to fan 4,000 batters, and he still ranks fourth on the all-time list.

"Lefty" made his Major League debut with St. Louis in 1965. He earned three All-Star selections with the Cardinals and won 20 games in 1971, but they traded him in 1972 after a contract dispute. That season, while playing for the last-place Phillies, Carlton turned in one of the most remarkable pitching performances of the modern era. Philadelphia managed only

Carpenter is one of today's top righties.

Carpenter, Chris

Chris Carpenter is a former first-round draft choice who overcame injury problems to become a Cy Young Award winner with the St. Louis Cardinals.

The Toronto Blue Jays chose the right-hander with the 15th overall pick of the 1993 draft, but it wasn't until Carpenter moved to the National League a decade later that he fulfilled his vast potential. He won 49 games in six seasons in Toronto beginning in 1997 and was the Blue Jays' Opening Day starter in 2002. He battled shoulder trouble much of the season, however, and was released at the end of the year.

After signing with the Cardinals in 2003, Carpenter did not make a Major League appearance that season while his shoulder healed. Then, in 2004, he won a career-best 15 games against only 5 losses. His pitching helped the Cardinals win the N.L. pennant. The next season, he was even better, going 21–5 and striking out 213 batters while posting an ERA of 2.83 to take top pitching honors in the National League. After another 15-win season in 2006, his injury troubles returned. Carpenter made only one start in '07 before undergoing Tommy John surgery on his throwing shoulder. That kept him on the shelf for the first half of 2008, too.

57 victories that year, but Carlton won 27 of them. He struck out 310 batters, posted a 1.97 ERA, and won the first of four Cy Young Awards in 11 seasons.

Carlton finished his career with several big-league teams past the age of 40, but his best seasons came in Philadelphia. In 14 full seasons with the Phillies from 1972 to 1985, he was an all-star seven times and won 20 or more games five times.

Carter, Gary

Gary Carter was a Hall-of-Fame catcher known for the youthful enthusiasm that he maintained throughout his 19-year big-league career.

Carter was just 20 years old when he first was called up to the Montreal Expos in September of 1974. "The Kid" made the All-Star Game in his official full rookie season in '75. In 1980, he drove in more than 100 runs (101) for the first of four times in his career and finished second in the National League MVP balloting. In 1985, when the Expos realized they wouldn't be able to afford to sign him again, Carter was traded to the Mets in exchange for four younger players. The next year, he drove in 105 runs and helped New York win the World Series. He had two homers and a Series-high nine RBI as New York beat Boston in seven games.

Throughout his career, Carter was as valuable to his team for his defense as for his hitting. Even though he was a part-time outfielder at first and did not become a full-time catcher until 1977, he was one of the best of his era behind the plate. In 1978, for instance, he was charged with just one passed ball—the fewest ever by a catcher who played more than 150 games.

Carter earned 11 All-Star selections in his career and twice was named the MVP of the game. He earned a spot in the Hall of Fame in 2003.

Cartwright, Alexander

Alexander Cartwright did not invent baseball, as he is sometimes credited. But he did earn the title of "Father of Modern Baseball" for his role in shaping the game as we know it today.

Baseball had been played in various formats before Cartwright organized the Knickerbocker Baseball Club of New York in 1845. He standardized the rag-tag game by placing the bases at 90 feet (27 m) apart and setting a regulation game at nine innings. He created fair and foul territory, set three outs as the accepted length of

■ *Carter first gained fame in Montreal, Canada.*

an inning, and made it illegal to put out runners by throwing the ball at them. It's important to note that other members of his club, notably a man named Doc Adams, should also be credited with helping create these new, more standard rules.

Later, Cartwright spread the word about baseball as he traveled to California during the Gold Rush. Eventually, he settled in Hawaii, where he became the fire chief of Honolulu and one of the state's leading citizens. In 1938, he was inducted into the Baseball Hall of Fame.

■ *Here it is: baseball's most famous catch.*

"Casey at the Bat"

"Casey at the Bat" is one of the most famous American poems, and not just among baseball fans. It is about a baseball player with the last name of Casey, a superstar player who is the last hope of the hometown "Mudville Nine" in the bottom of the ninth inning of a big game. But with his team trailing by two runs and men at second and third base, Casey strikes out to end the game.

The poem was written in 1888 by newspaperman Ernest Thayer and first published in the *San Francisco Examiner* in June that year. An actor named DeWolf Hopper became famous for reciting the poem onstage in New York for the first time in August of 1888 and for countless times after that. How often did he recite the famous poem? "How many times can best be numbered by the stars in the Milky Way," he once said.

Here's the final stanza to Ernest Thayer's poem, "Casey at the Bat":

Casey at the Bat

Oh, somewhere in this favored land the
*   sun is shining bright;*
The band is playing somewhere, and some-
*   where hearts are light,*
And somewhere men are laughing, and
*   somewhere children shout;*
But there is no joy in Mudville–mighty
*   Casey has struck out.*

The Catch

In baseball, "The Catch" refers to Willie Mays' over-the-shoulder grab of a long fly ball in the 1954 World Series. It is often considered the greatest defensive play in Major League Baseball history.

Mays was playing center field for the New York Giants in Game One in the spacious Polo Grounds when the Cleveland Indians' Vic Wertz came up to bat with two runners on base and the score tied 2–2. Wertz drilled a long fly ball to deep center—perhaps as much as 450 from home plate. Mays turned and sprinted toward the wall. He not only made the catch with his back to the plate,

■ *Catchers need gear for protection from balls and runners.*

but he also whirled and threw the ball back to the infield.

Mays' great catch preserved the tie score, and the Giants eventually won in 10 innings, 5–2. They went on to sweep the Indians in four games and win the Series.

Catcher

A catcher is the defensive player who is positioned directly behind home plate. He is the only player on the pitching team who does not line up in fair territory. In scorekeeping, the catcher is designated by position number 2.

Catchers must have the strength and stamina to withstand the rigors of their position. They are constantly in and out of a crouch to receive pitches, and sometimes must physically block home plate from approaching runners. Catchers also must have a strong arm in order to throw out potential base stealers.

Catchers are usually chosen for their position because of their defensive skills. A good-hitting catcher, though, is a big bonus for his team.

Catcher's Gear

A catcher's gear is sometimes referred to as the "Tools of Ignorance." That's a tongue-in-cheek reference sometimes attributed to Bill Dickey, a Hall-of-Fame catcher for the Yankees from 1928 to 1946, and sometimes to Muddy Ruel, another big-league catcher from 1915 to 1934.

The catcher's gear includes a mask, chest protector, and shin guards. A catcher's gear also includes a specially padded glove. In the 1870s, catchers were the first players to wear gloves in the field.

Catcher's equipment has evolved over the years in response to safety concerns. Masks originally were metal cages that covered just the face. Today, however, larger masks include throat guards, which did not appear until the 1970s, and helmets on the back of the head. Some catchers prefer to wear a hockey-style goaltender's mask for even greater protection. Shin guards now also cover the bottom of the thigh and top of the feet. Catchers all wear a protective athletic cup, as well.

■ *Center fielders have a lot of grass to cover in the outfield.*

Center Field

 The center fielder is the player who is positioned in the outfield between the right fielder and the left fielder. He is basically on a direct line behind the catcher and pitcher, although he will shift to the right or left depending on the batter, his pitcher's strengths, the game situation, and other factors.

The center fielder is usually a team's best defensive outfielder. He has to cover more ground than the other outfielders. The general rule of thumb is that the center fielder has the responsibility of catching any ball he can get to. Sometimes, though, it is his job to call who will make the catch.

Chadwick, Henry

Every baseball fan who enjoys reading box scores on the Internet or in the morning newspaper should say thanks to Henry Chadwick. In the 1860s, he was the journalist who first developed the modern statistical summary of a baseball game.

Chadwick was responsible for a lot more than the box score, however. He also introduced statistics such as batting average and ERA and worked hard to promote the young sport of baseball. A native of England, he helped make baseball America's favorite pastime by writing instruction manuals, editing yearly baseball guides, and serving on rules committees. He was inducted into the National Baseball Hall of Fame in 1938.

Changeup

A changeup is a type of pitch. Sometimes, it is called a "change of pace." As the name suggests, it is a change in the speed, of the ball: It is slower than a fastball. It is difficult for a batter because it is thrown with the same motion as a regular fastball, so it is hard to see coming.

A pitcher with a good changeup can be very effective because he keeps the batter guessing how quickly the ball will get to home plate. (Sometimes, that's called keeping a hitter "off balance.")

Charleston, Oscar

Oscar Charleston was one of the greatest players in the history of the Negro Leagues. In fact, he is often considered the greatest player in Negro League history.

Charleston was a center fielder who was compared to Ty Cobb for his base running, to Tris Speaker for his fielding, and to Babe Ruth for his hitting—all three of them, of course, are in the Baseball Hall of Fame.

■ *This batter can still stop, or "check," his swing and let the pitch go by.*

Charleston was voted into the Hall by the Negro Leagues committee in 1976.

Charleston was just 18 when he began his pro career with the Indianapolis ABCs in 1915. He went on to spend 40 years in the Negro Leagues as a player and/or manager until his death in 1954. Few official statistics exist from his playing days, but he was a regular .300 hitter who once batted an astounding .434 for the St. Louis Giants in the Negro National League in 1921. The Indianapolis native was so fast that he was nicknamed "The Hoosier Comet."

Check Swing

A check swing is when a batter begins to swing and then changes his mind. He stops his swing, or "checks" it, before it crosses home plate. If a batter makes contact with the ball on a check swing, it

continued on page 67

Wrigley Field has been the home of the Cubs since 1916.

Chicago Cubs

The Chicago Cubs, one of baseball's top teams in the early 1900s, have not won a World Series in 100 years—a stretch some say is due in part to a famous curse. Despite the team's long time without a title, though, Cubs' followers are among baseball's most loyal.

The curse came in 1945, when a fan tried to bring a pet goat into a World Series game. They were prevented from entering the ballpark. In response, the man put a hex on the team, saying it would never win another World Series. Sure enough, the Cubs haven't. They haven't even won the N.L. since.

The Cubs didn't always struggle to produce championships, though. The franchise officially began in the National Association in the early 1870s. The National Association was the highest level of professional play at the time. In 1876, Chicago, then known as the White Stockings, joined the newly formed National League. Immediately, the club was a winner. From 1880 to 1886, the team won five titles in seven seasons.

First baseman Cap Anson was the franchise's earliest star, and was the player-manager from 1879–1897. The franchise got the name Cubs in 1903.

In 1906, the team won a big-league-record 116 games and the first of four National League pennants in five seasons. The 1907 and 1908 teams won the World Series. Those Cubs' teams featured the famous double-play combination of Joe Tinker, Johnny Evers, and Frank Chance—"Tinker to Evers to Chance"—and the pitching of Hall-of-Famer Mordecai "Three-Finger" Brown.

CHICAGO CUBS

LEAGUE: **NATIONAL**

DIVISION: **CENTRAL**

YEAR FOUNDED: **1871**

CURRENT COLORS:
BLUE, WHITE, AND RED

STADIUM (CAPACITY):
**WRIGLEY FIELD
(41,160)**

ALL-TIME RECORD
(THROUGH 2008):
10.082–9,523

WORLD SERIES TITLES
(MOST RECENT):
2 (1908)

In 1916, the Cubs moved into Wrigley Field, which is still their home. Wrigley Field, which is older than every other ballpark in the Major Leagues except Boston's Fenway Park, didn't have lights until 1988. The team played only day games until then.

Chicago won half a dozen N.L. pennants from 1918 to 1945, but always fell short in the World Series. The Cubs had lots of great players, though, such as outfielder Hack Wilson, who set a big-league record that still stands when he drove in 191 runs in 1930.

In the late 1950s, shortstop Ernie Banks ("Mr. Cub") won back-to-back N.L. MVP awards despite playing on last-place teams. In 1959, he was joined on the Cubs by another future Hall-of-Famer, Billy Williams. The smooth-hitting outfielder played in Chicago through the 1974 season.

Second baseman Ryne Sandberg was the star of a couple of playoff teams in the 1980s, and outfielder Sammy Sosa arrived via trade with Chicago White Sox in 1992. In 1998, he slugged 66 home runs—that would have been a big-league record except St. Louis' Mark McGwire belted 70 that year.

Also in 1998, rookie Kerry Wood arrived and struck out 20 batters in a single game.

Five years later, in 2003, Chicago looked as if it would finally break its World Series jinx. After building a three-games-to-one lead over Florida in the N.L. Championship

■ *Kosuke Fukudome joined the Cubs in 2008.*

Series, the Cubs led 3–0 in the eighth inning of Game Six at home. With fans ready to celebrate, the Cubs, incredibly, blew the lead and went on to lose the Series.

Manager Lou Piniella, who took over in 2007, used an offense led by third baseman Aramis Ramirez, first baseman Derek Lee, and outfielder Alfonso Soriano. And he built a pitching staff around ace Carlos Zambrano.

Piniella's first team made the playoffs. His second team, in 2008, won a division title. Though they lost in the NLDS, the Cubs hope that the end of the curse is in sight.

Chicago White Sox

Unlike their crosstown rival Chicago Cubs of the National League, the American League's Chicago White Sox never had a curse placed on them. But it took the team 86 years to erase the painful memories of the biggest scandal in baseball history. That was the "Black Sox" scandal of 1919; after that, Chicago did not win a World Series until 2005.

■ *Joe Jackson was an all-time great hitter.*

Before the scandal, the White Sox were one of the young A.L.'s most successful clubs. They started when former big-league first baseman Charles Comiskey moved a minor-league team to Chicago. The White Sox joined the American League in 1901.

At the time, the White Sox were called the White Stockings after the original name of the N.L.'s Cubs. Newspapers shortened White Stockings to White Sox, and the new name stuck. In 1906, the two Chicago teams met in the World Series. Though the Cubs had won a record 116 games during the season, the White Sox took the Series four games to two for their first championship.

In 1917, the White Sox fielded a powerful team. Behind the hitting of "Shoeless Joe" Jackson and the pitching of Eddie Cicotte, Chicago won 100 games. The White Sox beat the Giants in six games to win the World Series for the second time. It would be a long wait for championship No. 3.

Most White Sox fans thought the team's third title would come in 1919. Jackson hit .351 that year, while Eddie Collins batted .319. Cicotte (29 wins) and Lefty Williams (23) combined to win 52 games. Chicago was heavily favored to win the World Series over the N.L.'s Cincinnati Reds.

Strangely, though, some of the talented White Sox players made fielding errors, pitching mistakes, or baserunning blunders.

Rumors spread that some White Sox players had been paid by gamblers to lose on purpose. Later, it was revealed that seven players, including Jackson and Cicotte, had accepted bribes. Another player knew about the bribes but did not report them. The eight players were banned from the sport for life.

The fault was with the players who accepted the bribes, of course. But Comiskey's reputation suffered, too. He came across as a penny-pincher who underpaid his players and sometimes didn't even have their uniforms washed, just to save on the laundry bill. Comiskey, who died in 1931, never saw his team win another pennant.

From 1921–1951, Chicago lost more games than it won. Finally, in 1951, the White Sox began a better streak: They had winning records 17 seasons in a row.

The 1959 team nearly broke the White Sox' championship drought. That team didn't have much power on offense, so it utilized its great speed and pitching; they were nicknamed the "Go-Go Sox." Shortstop Luis Aparicio led the league with 56 steals, pitcher Early Wynn topped the circuit with 22 victories, and Chicago won a lot of low-scoring games. In the World Series, though, the Dodgers won in six games.

That was as close as the White Sox got until 2005. There were some good teams, like the 1983, 1993, and 2000 squads that won division championships. And there were some great players,

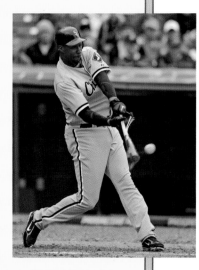

■ *White Sox slugger Jermaine Dye.*

such as first baseman two-time MVP Frank "The Big Hurt" Thomas. He hit better than .300, scored more than 100 runs, drove in at least 100 runs, and walked more than 100 times for seven seasons in a row in the 1990s.

By 2005, though, the stars were first baseman Paul Konerko and outfielder Jermaine Dye. The White Sox finished six games ahead of the Cleveland Indians in the A.L. Central race, then won 11 of 12 games in the postseason. They swept the Houston Astros in four games to win the World Series. It had been a long wait for Chicago fans.

CHICAGO WHITE SOX

LEAGUE: **AMERICAN**

DIVISION: **CENTRAL**

YEAR FOUNDED: **1901**

CURRENT COLORS: **BLACK AND GRAY**

STADIUM (CAPACITY): **U.S. CELLULAR FIELD (40,615)**

ALL-TIME RECORD (THROUGH 2008): **8,461–8,256**

WORLD SERIES TITLES (MOST RECENT): **3 (2005)**

■ *Rose (left), Bench (center), and Morgan led the Reds.*

Cincinnati Reds

The Cincinnati Reds have won five World Series and nine pennants since joining the National League in 1890. The franchise's best era came in the 1970s, when it was the top team in the league and became known as the "Big Red Machine."

The history of the Reds, though, goes back to the roots of professional baseball. In 1869, the Reds (or the Red Stockings, as they officially were called then) fielded the first all-professional team.

Seven years later, the franchise was an original member of the National League—

although it was eventually kicked out of the league for selling beer at its games and renting out its ballpark on Sundays. When the American Association was formed in 1882 as a big-league alternative to the N.L., the Reds joined. Cincinnati won the first American Association champion-ship, but jumped back to the National League in 1890.

The Reds had a handful of good seasons, but they didn't break through for a pennant until 1919. Even then, their World Series victory over the Chicago White Sox was tainted. That was the year of the famous "Black Sox" scandal, when Chicago players were accused of losing games on purpose.

Over the next 50 years, the Reds man-aged to win the World Series only one time. That came in 1940, when they won 100 games during the regular season, then edged the Detroit Tigers in seven games.

The team had plenty of great stars and memorable moments in that time, however. In 1938, for instance, Cincinnati's Johnny Vander Meer became the first—and still only—pitcher in big-league history to pitch no-hit games in back-to-back starts. That same year, catcher Ernie Lombardi was named the N.L. MVP. Pitcher Bucky Walters won the award the next season, and in 1940 first baseman Frank McCormick was honored. That made the Reds the first team to have three different players win the award in consecutive years.

In 1956, the Reds added superstar Frank Robinson, who would go on to become one of the greatest hitters in baseball history. Robinson was the N.L. MVP in 1961 and the A.L. MVP in 1966 (while with Baltimore), and was inducted into the Hall of Fame.

Then came the 1970s. It was the greatest decade in Reds' history. Manager Sparky Anderson's batting lineup much of that time included stars such as catcher Johnny Bench; infielders Joe Morgan, Pete Rose, Tony Perez, and Dave Concepcion; and outfielders George Foster and Ken Griffey.

The Big Red Machine won 102 games and the N.L. pennant in 1970, but it was just warming up. Cincinnati forged an amazing 108–54 record in 1975 and won the World Series. The Reds' seven-game victory over the Red Sox that year—Morgan drove in the winning run in the ninth inning of the final game—is considered one of the greatest Fall Classics. The next year, the Reds swept the Yankees to win again.

Cincinnati has not been as dominant since, but has had some very good teams. In 1985, Rose was the player-manager and set a Major League record with his 4,192nd career hit. Rose helped develop some great young stars such as shortstop Barry Larkin and outfielders Eric Davis and Paul O'Neill. Those players helped new manager Lou Piniella's club win the World Series in 1990 with an upset of the favored Oakland Athletics.

■ *Adam Dunn: 270 HRs from 2001–08.*

The decade of the 2000s has not been so kind to the Reds. They welcomed Ken Griffey Jr., the son of the Big Red Machine outfielder, in 2000, and the team moved into the beautiful Great American Ballpark in 2003. Those moves did not translate into on-field success, although Griffey made headlines in 2008 when reached 600 career home runs (before being traded to the Chicago White Sox).

CINCINNATI REDS

LEAGUE: **NATIONAL**

DIVISION: **CENTRAL**

YEAR FOUNDED: **1869**

CURRENT COLORS:
RED AND BLACK

STADIUM (CAPACITY):
GREAT AMERICAN BALL PARK (42,941)

ALL-TIME RECORD
(THROUGH 2008):
9,746–9,464

WORLD SERIES TITLES
(MOST RECENT):
5 (1990)

Clemente, Roberto

Roberto Clemente spent 18 seasons in a Hall-of-Fame career with the Pittsburgh Pirates beginning in 1955. He batted .317 and hit 240 home runs, and his rifle arm and terrific baseball instincts made him one of the greatest all-around outfielders of all time. His impact on the sport reached beyond the diamond, however. Clemente was the first Latin American-born player inducted into the Hall of Fame, and because of his commitment to the community and to humanitarian efforts, Major League Baseball's highest service award is named for him.

Clemente was a teenage star in his native Puerto Rico. He was just 20 years old when he joined the Pirates in 1955. By 1960, he was an All-Star, and in 1961, he hit .351 to win the first of four career batting titles. He also earned the first of 12 straight Gold Gloves that season. His best season came in 1966, when he hit .317 and posted career bests of 29 home runs, 119 RBI, and 105 runs scored en route to winning National League MVP honors.

The Pirates won exciting seven-game World Series in both 1960 and 1971, in large part to Clemente's clutch hitting. He batted safely in all 14 of those games, hitting .414 overall. He was named the MVP of the 1971 World Series.

On his final at-bat of the 1972 season, Clemente got his 3,000th career hit. It turned out to be the final plate appearance of his career. On December 31 that year, Clemente was killed in a plane crash while bring relief supplies to earthquake victims in Nicaragua.

■ *Clemente was one of the best all-around players.*

is treated as any other swing. If he doesn't make contact, though, the umpire determines if the check swing went more than halfway through the hitting zone. If it did, it is ruled the same as a full swing, which means it is a strike. Sometimes the home-plate umpire asks the base umpires for help to determine if a check swing should be ruled a full swing.

Chicago Cubs

Please see pages 60–61.

Chicago White Sox

Please see pages 62–63.

Cincinnati Reds

Please see pages 64–65.

Cleanup hitter

The cleanup hitter is the fourth batter in a team's starting lineup. It is usually a team's best power hitter. He is put into that spot in the lineup on the theory that he will come up with men on and "clean up," or drive home, the runners on base.

Cleats

Cleats are the shoes that baseball players wear. They feature a series of metal or plastic tabs, or "spikes," that grip the dirt and grass. Most Major League teams currently play on natural turf, but in the 1970s, many artificial surfaces were in use.

■ *"The Rocket" roared to seven Cy Young Awards.*

That led to a new type of baseball cleat that included hundreds of small bumps on the bottom of the shoe for better traction.

Clemens, Roger

Roger Clemens built a reputation as one of the greatest pitchers in Major League history over the course of a long career that lasted nearly a quarter of a century from 1984 to 2007. But his reputation

continued on page 70

Cleveland Indians

Long-suffering fans of the Cleveland Indians are still looking for the team's first World Series championship since the 1948 season. The Indians have won only two titles in their history.

Cleveland began as an original member of the American League in 1901. The team was called the Blues back then because of the color of their uniforms. The next year, they were called the Bronchos and they

■ *"Rapid Robert" Feller of the Indians.*

traded for their first star: second baseman Nap Lajoie (lah-ZHO-way).

Lajoie not only was one of the best players in the American League, but he was a great leader, too. In 1905, he took over as the team's player-manager. Lajoie, who eventually was the first second baseman to make it into the Hall of Fame, became so popular in Cleveland that the team became known as the "Naps" as long as he was with the team (through 1914). In 1915, Cleveland finally became the Indians.

(Why Indians? In 1914, it was the winning entry in a contest to name the team. It was in honor of Louis "Chief" Sockalexis. He was a legend in Cleveland while playing for the N.L.'s Cleveland Spiders in the 1890s and the first Native American to play pro baseball.)

As good as Lajoie was, he couldn't carry the team to its first pennant. That pennant didn't come until 1920, when Tris Speaker—another player-manager and another future Hall of Famer—batted .388 for the A.L. champs. In the World Series, Cleveland routed Brooklyn five games to two (the World Series was best-of-nine games then). In that World Series, Cleveland second baseman Bill Wambsganss made an unassisted triple play—the only one to come in the Fall Classic.

In 1936, Bob Feller arrived. "Rapid Robert" was only 17 years old when he made his big-league debut, but he already was one of the league's hardest throwers. In 1938, Feller made the All-Star Game for the first of eight times. In 1939, he led the American League in wins (24) for the first of six times. And in 1940, he pitched the only Opening-Day no-hitter in history (against the White Sox).

In 1948, Feller won 19 games and led the league in strikeouts for the seventh time. Shortstop Lou Boudreau, another player-manager, batted .355 and earned A.L. MVP honors. The Indians won the pennant, then beat the Boston Braves in six games in the World Series. Cleveland hasn't won another title since.

It's not that they haven't come close, though. In 1954, Feller was joined by two other future Hall-of-Fame pitchers—Bob Lemon and Early Wynn. Out-fielder Larry Doby, another future Hall of Famer, led the league with 32 homers and 126 RBI. The Indians won a club-record 111 games, but lost four games in a row to the New York Giants in the World Series.

In 1975, the Indians made news when DH Frank Robinson, who was still an active player, became Major League Baseball's first African-American manager.

In 1995, while play-ing in new Jacobs Field (now Progressive Field and still one of the best of the newer ball-parks in the Majors), the Indians began a string of five consecu-tive division champion-ships under manager Mike Hargrove. With outfielder Albert Belle slugging 50 home runs, the Indians won the A.L. pennant, but lost the World Series to the Atlanta Braves.

■ *Young star Grady Sizemore.*

Two years later, the Indians made it back to the Fall Classic. They were three outs away from win-ning Game Seven, but the Florida Marlins tied the game in the ninth, and then won it in the 11th.

Behind new hitting stars such as designated hitter Travis Hafner and outfielder Grady Sizemore, the Indians have continued to field good teams in the 2000s. All that is left for fans of "The Tribe" is for the team to capture that elusive World Series title.

CLEVELAND INDIANS

LEAGUE: **AMERICAN**

DIVISION: **CENTRAL**

YEAR FOUNDED: **1901**

CURRENT COLORS:
NAVY BLUE AND RED

STADIUM (CAPACITY):
PROGRESSIVE FIELD (43,345)

ALL-TIME RECORD (THROUGH 2008):
8,557–8,177

WORLD SERIES TITLES (MOST RECENT): **2 (1948)**

■ *A base coach (No. 3) helps baserunners.*

has been hurt in recent years over accusations that he used performance-enhancing drugs. He has repeatedly denied all of those charges.

Clemens was a first-round draft choice of the Boston Red Sox in June of 1983 and was in the big leagues less than one year later. He won nine games as a rookie and seven in an injury-shortened season in 1985 before becoming a star in '86. In his first full season as a starter, "Rocket" won his first 14 decisions en route to a 24–4 record. He struck out 238 batters, compiled an ERA of 2.48, and won the first of a record seven Cy Young Awards as the best pitcher in his league. He also earned A.L. MVP honors that year.

Clemens went on to win 192 games in 13 seasons in Boston, but he was just getting warmed up. He would go on to pitch three seasons in Toronto, five with the Yankees—he was a remarkable 20–3 at age 38 in 2001—and three in Houston before finishing up with one more season for the Yankees in 2007.

The laundry list of Clemens' accomplishments is remarkable. He won 20 or more games six times and earned 11 All-Star selections. His 354 career victories rank eighth on the all-time list. His 4,672 strikeouts stand second only to Nolan Ryan. He pitched for six pennant-winning teams and two World Series champions.

Clemens' incredible success, work ethic, and competitive drive made him a hero to many baseball fans. Whether or not his reputation survives the allegations of performance-enhancing drug use remains to be seen.

Cleveland Indians

Please see pages 68–69.

Closer

The closer is a relief pitcher who specializes in the getting the final few outs of a game in which his team has the lead. Closers are the pitchers who earn the most saves.

Closers are not limited only to save situations. Occasionally, a closer will enter a game in the late innings or extra innings to preserve a tie, or just to get some work in during a lopsided contest. But some managers prefer to use their closer only in the ninth inning of a close game.

In 2006, Bruce Sutter became the first modern closer—a player who spent his entire career in relief and as a save specialist—to make it into the Hall of Fame.

Coach

In baseball, a coach assists the manager. It is the manager who is responsible for making all on-field decisions, such as who plays what position, where each player bats in the lineup, and when to remove a pitcher from the game. But each manager also has several coaches. They specialize in working with hitters or pitchers, or assisting on the bench or in the bullpen.

Each team also has a first-base coach and a third-base coach who are on the field (in foul territory) when the team is at bat. They relay instructional signs from the manager to the hitter and base runners, and help runners decide when to advance or stop at a base through arm motions and verbal signals.

Cobb, Ty

No discussion of the greatest players in baseball history is complete without Ty Cobb's name included. In fact, in 1936 the former Tigers' outfielder was one of the five players to make up the first class of the Baseball Hall of Fame. (Walter Johnson, Christy Mathewson, Babe Ruth, and Honus Wagner were the others.)

In 24 big-league seasons from 1905 to 1928 (the final two came with the Philadelphia Athletics after 24 years in Detroit), the "Georgia Peach" batted a record .366 overall—only a handful of players since have hit for a higher average in any single season. He had 4,189 hits, scored 2,246 runs, and legged out 297 triples. Eighty years after his final game, those figures still rank second on Major League Baseball's all-time list. His 892 steals rank fourth, and his 1,937 RBI are seventh.

■ *Some experts call Cobb the best player ever.*

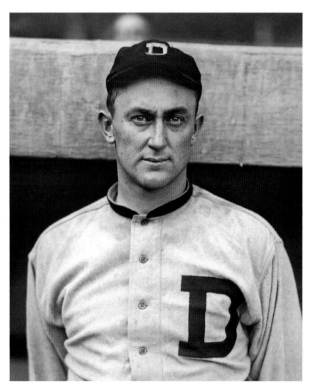

71

Cobb won 12 batting titles in his career, including eight in a nine-season span from 1911 to 1919. In 1911, he batted a career-best .420 and won the first American League MVP award.

And yet, statistics tell only part of the story. Cobb's fierce competitiveness set him apart. He disrupted opposing pitchers and players with aggressive play that does not show up in the box score.

Cochrane, Mickey

By batting .320 for 13 big-league seasons from 1925 to 1937, Mickey Cochrane compiled a higher career average than any other catcher in history. He also was a standout backstop who led all American League catchers in putouts six times and in assists and double plays twice each. He was inducted into the Hall of Fame in 1947.

Beyond the numbers, Cochrane was one of baseball's great leaders. Philadelphia manager Connie Mack recognized that early on and bought an entire Pacific Coast League franchise in 1924 just to obtain the catching star. Cochrane soon helped Mack's Athletics win back-to-back World Series in 1929 and 1930. (The '31 squad won the pennant, but lost the World Series.) In 1934, Cochrane became the Tigers' player-manager. He led Detroit to the 1934 pennant, then to a thrilling World Series victory over the Cubs in '35.

Cochrane scored the winning run with two outs in the bottom of the ninth inning of the decisive Game Six that year.

Cochrane's given first name was Gordon, but he went by the nickname Mickey. Another future Hall of Famer, Yankees great Mickey Mantle, was named after him: Cochrane was the favorite player of Mantle's dad.

College Baseball

College baseball has existed since 1859, although baseball rules were not standardized then, and the game was significantly different than it is now.

The most important development in the growth of college baseball came in 1947, when the National Collegiate Athletic Association (NCAA) first played the College World Series in Kalamazoo, Michigan. Two years later, the CWS moved to Omaha, Nebraska, where it has been a fixture at Rosenblatt Stadium ever since. Southern California has won the most CWS championship, with 12 entering 2009. Texas has six titles, and Arizona State and LSU have five each. Fresno State University was the 2008 NCAA champion.

USA Baseball is the national governing body of amateur baseball. Its annual Golden Spikes Award annually is presented to the top amateur player in the country (making it roughly the equivalent of college football's Heisman Trophy).

Collins, Eddie

 No other second baseman in big-league history played in more games than Eddie Collins. The Philadelphia Athletics' and Chicago White Sox' star played in 2,826 games (including 2,650 games at second) in a 25-year career from 1906 to 1930.

In those 2,826 games, Collins amassed 3,315 hits, which still ranked 10th on the all-time list in 2008. Once on base, he knew how to get around, too: His 744 career steals is seventh among all players in big-league history, and his 1,821 runs are 15th.

Collins had a .333 career batting average that included seasons of .372 (1920), .365 (1911), and .360 (1923). Remarkably, though, he never won a batting title—his career overlapped that of Ty Cobb, who hogged most of the hitting crowns in that span.

Collins had a leg up on Cobb in one category, though. While Cobb never played on a World Series champion, Collins helped the Athletics to three titles: 1910, 1911, and 1913. In 1915, he was sold to the White Sox; two years later, he helped that club win the World Series.

Collins, Jimmy

 Although Jimmy Collins' batting statistics pale in comparison to those of

■ *Fresno State's Bulldogs celebrate a college title in 2008.*

many other Hall of Famers—he played in the Dead Ball Era—he is widely considered one of the greatest third basemen in history. In 14 seasons, he led his league's third basemen in putouts five times, in assists four times, and in double plays twice. He was particularly adept at fielding bunts and throwing out runners.

Collins made his pro debut for the National League's Boston Beaneaters in 1895, although he was loaned to the Louisville Colonels for most of that season. He returned to Boston in 1896, and he hit .349

continued on page 76

73

Larry Walker was a N.L. MVP with Colorado.

Colorado Rockies

From the beginning as an expansion team in 1993, the Rockies have enjoyed enormous enthusiasm from their fans in the Rocky Mountain region. In 2007, the team rewarded those fans with the first pennant in franchise history.

That the Rockies were a big hit in Denver was no surprise. That city's fans long had supported minor-league baseball in the area.

In the Rockies' first season, the team drew 4,483,350 fans. That was a new Major League record.

The Rockies weren't just a big hit at the gate, however. They were a big hit—literally—on the field. In fact, in the very first at-bat in a regular season game by a Rockies' player, infielder Eric Young hit a home run.

The Rockies' first hitting star was Andres Galarraga. The first baseman always had been an excellent hitter. But with the Rockies, he batted a league-leading .370 with 98 RBI in 1993. In five seasons with Colorado, he averaged 34 home runs and 116 RBI per year.

After Galarraga came such sluggers as Larry Walker, Todd Helton, and Matt Holliday, the latest hitting star.

Those players put up some amazing numbers. In 1997, for instance, Walker hit .366 while slugging 49 home runs and driving in 130 runs. He stole 33 bases, too, and was named the league's MVP. Helton was the rookie of the year the following season, and in 2000, he batted .372 with 42 home runs and 147 RBI; in 2001, he batted .336 with 49 homers and 146 RBI. Holliday arrived on the scene in 2004 and was an All-Star by '06. In 2007, he hit .340 with 36 home runs and 137 RBI.

Notice a trend here? It's been all about hitting in Colorado. In the 15 seasons from 1993 to 2007, the Rockies led the league in scoring five times. Scores of their home games were often 12–8 or 9–7. While the Rockies' hitters have historically flourished, their pitchers have not. In those same 15 seasons, Colorado pitchers allowed the most runs in the National League 10 times.

Much of the reason for this is because of the Rockies' home park. Coors Field lies one mile above sea level—Denver is called the "Mile-High City"—and baseballs travel farther in the thin air.

In recent years, the team has tried to even things out a bit for the pitchers by storing baseballs in a humidor, a special room in which the temperature and air pressure can be controlled. In theory, that keeps the balls from drying out in the thin air and keeps batters from routinely hitting them out of the park.

Whether it was the humidor or not, the Rockies' pitching was much better in 2007, and that led to a great year. After never winning more than 83 games in any season and making the play-offs just once—a quick exit in the Division Series in 1995—Colorado won 90 games and its first N.L. pennant.

As late as September 15, the Rockies were in fourth place in the Western Division. But Colorado won 11 games in a row and 14 out of the next 15 games. That was good enough to earn a wild-card playoff berth.

■ *Todd Helton, 2000 batting champ.*

In the playoffs, the Rockies still couldn't be beat. They swept the Phillies in three games, then swept the Diamondbacks in four games in the NLCS. Closer Manny Corpas got Arizona's Eric Byrnes to ground out for the final out in Game Four and send the Rockies to the World Series for the first time.

Although the championship dream died when the Red Sox swept Colorado in the World Series, the Rockies and their fans were still feeling a Mile High after a magical season.

COLORADO ROCKIES

LEAGUE: **NATIONAL**

DIVISION: **WEST**

YEAR FOUNDED: **1993**

CURRENT COLORS:
BLACK, SILVER, AND PURPLE

STADIUM (CAPACITY):
COORS FIELD (50,445)

ALL-TIME RECORD (THROUGH 2008):
1,189–1,341

WORLD SERIES TITLES
NONE

■ *Today's Chicago White Sox play in a new version of Comiskey Park, now named for a sponsor.*

for the Beaneaters the next year. In 1897, he led the N.L. with 15 home runs.

In 1901, Collins became the player-manager of the Boston franchise in the new American League. Two years later, he led Boston to the league pennant and into the first World Series against Pittsburgh. Collins' team from the fledgling league upset the Pirates five games to three.

Colorado Rockies

Please see pages 74–75.

Comiskey, Charles

Beginning with his rookie season at first base for the American Association's St. Louis Brown Stockings in 1882

until his death in 1931, Charles Comiskey spent 50 seasons in pro baseball as a player, manager, and owner.

As a player, Comiskey's greatest claim to fame was playing off the bag at first base. Most first basemen of the era began each play with a foot on the bag, but they soon copied the successful Comiskey, who became St. Louis' player-manager in his second season.

Comiskey's on-field career ended in 1894, but he soon embarked on a long tenure as a team owner. Around the turn of the century, he was instrumental in helping Ban Johnson start the American League by purchasing a Western League franchise and moving it to Chicago. Comiskey's White

Sox went on to win the American League pennant in its first season in 1901 and three more times before 1920.

The White Sox' last pennant winner under Comiskey, though, was the infamous "Black Sox" team of 1919 that lost the World Series. Eight players from that team were accused of losing games on purpose. Some of them later blamed Comiskey's penny-pinching for their willingness to take bribes. Comiskey was embarrassed in the scandal, but still was inducted into the Hall of Fame in 1939.

Comiskey Park

Comiskey Park was the home of the American League's Chicago White Sox from 1910 through 1990. It originally was called White Sox Park before being named in honor of longtime White Sox owner and A.L. pioneer Charles Comiskey.

Major League Baseball's first All-Star Game was played at Comiskey Park in 1933. In 1960, then-owner Bill Veeck installed the most unique feature in Comiskey Park: an exploding scoreboard. It featured several pinwheels inspired by a pinball machine, and shot off fireworks after every White Sox home run.

The first Comiskey Park closed in 1990. The White Sox moved into New Comiskey Park in 1991. It is now called U.S. Cellular Field after a corporate sponsor purchased the naming rights.

Commissioner

The Commissioner of Baseball is the highest-ranking executive in the sport. Each team in baseball is owned separately, but the Commissioner's office oversees those 30 ownership groups. That office also negotiates labor contracts, makes the annual schedule, and is in charge of the umpiring crews.

The Commissioner position was created in 1920 following the "Black Sox Scandal." Before that, a three-man commission made baseball decisions. After the scandal, though, baseball turned to an iron-willed former federal judge named Kenesaw Mountain Landis in an effort to regain

■ *Bud Selig has been commissioner since 1992.*

credibility with the public. Landis demanded—and got—complete and unlimited authority. The owners agreed, and Landis served as Commissioner for 24 years.

Former Milwaukee Brewers owner Bud Selig entered his 18th year as the Commissioner of Baseball in 2009. That includes a period from 1992 to 1998 when he officially was the "Acting Commissioner." Baseball owners then voted him to the position on a full-time basis.

Cooperstown

Cooperstown is a village in the state of New York, located in Otsego County, that houses the National Baseball Hall of Fame and Museum.

COMMISSIONERS OF BASEBALL

NAME	YEARS
Kenesaw Mountain Landis	1920–1944
A.B. "Happy" Chandler Sr.	1945–1951
Ford Frick	1951–1965
William Eckert	1965–68
Bowie Kuhn	1969–1984
Peter Ueberroth	1984–89
Bart Giamatti	1989
Fay Vincent	1989–1992
Bud Selig	1992–present

For many years, baseball was believed to have been invented by U.S. Gen. Abner Doubleday on a field in Cooperstown, 100 years before the Hall opened its doors in 1939. Modern research has proven that false, though the "Doubleday Myth" remains part of baseball legend.

Cox, Bobby

Bobby Cox is the highly successful manager of the National League's Atlanta Braves. He was in his 31st season as a big-league manager in 2008. His 2,307 wins entering 2009 ranked fourth on baseball's all-time list.

An infielder with the Yankees in the late 1960s, Cox was only 36 years old when he took over as the Braves' manager for the first time in the 1978 season. In four years, though, he was unable to lift Atlanta out of the bottom half of its division.

■ *Bobby Cox, a manager for more than 30 years.*

He had more success in Toronto, where he took over a former expansion franchise that was still in its infancy in 1982. The Blue Jays gradually improved under Cox until they won 99 games in 1985 and won their first division title.

Cox was back in Atlanta the next season as the general manager, but he returned to the field in 1990. He's been at the helm ever since, and oversaw an unprecedented string of 14 consecutive division titles from 1991 to 2005. (There were no division winners in the strike-shortened 1994 season.) The Braves won five National League pennants in that span, and the 1995 squad beat the Cleveland Indians in six games to win the World Series.

Crawford, Carl

Carl Crawford is an All-Star outfielder for the American League's Tampa Bay Rays. He is a classic "five-tool" standout who can hit for average, hit for power, run, field, and throw well. Baseball scouts look for these tools when finding young players, and Crawford has a full tool cabinet!

Crawford was only 20 years old when he made his big-league debut for Tampa Bay in the summer of 2002. He stole 55 bases in his first full season in 2003 to lead the American League, then topped the circuit again with 59 steals in '04. That year, despite playing for a woeful Devil Rays' team (they have since shortened their name

■ *Crawford is an exciting player to watch.*

to the Rays), he made the All-Star Game for the first time. Crawford also topped the league in steals in 2006 (with 58) and '07 (50), another All-Star year.

Crawford is much more than just a speedster, though. Despite batting leadoff most of the time for Tampa, he also drove in a career-best 81 runs in 2005, then clubbed 18 home runs the next season. Crawford's batting average improved each season of his career before peaking at .315 in 2007.

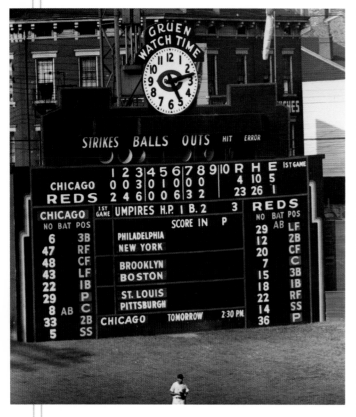

■ *A good view of the Crosley Field scoreboard.*

Crosley Field

The Cincinnati Reds played their home games at Crosley Field from 1912 until June of 1970. It originally was known as Redland Field before being renamed in honor of Reds owner Powel Crosley in 1933.

Major League Baseball's All-Star Game was played at Crosley Field in 1938 and 1953. Along with being the home of stars such as Ernie Lombardi, Ted Kluszewski, and Johnny Bench, Crosley Field also was the site of the big leagues' first night game, when the Reds hosted the Philadelphia Phillies on May 24, 1935.

Cuba, Baseball in

Baseball in Cuba has a long history that dates to 1866, when visiting American sailors and workers introduced the game there. Twelve years later, just two years after the National League began play in the United States, Cuba's first professional league began.

That league thrived in the first half of the 20th century, as many American players spent their offseasons in the Cuban Winter League. But in 1961, after the Cuban revolution, dictator Fidel Castro outlawed professional sports.

Communist Cuba continued to field strong national teams, however. Cuba won Olympic gold medals in 1992, 1996, and 2004, and the 2006 national squad finished in second place at the inaugural World Baseball Classic.

Castro was a huge baseball fan who likely pitched in intramural competition at the University of Havana. But he did not try out with Major League Baseball's Washington Senators, which is a myth that has been widely circulated.

Several current Major League stars have made their way from Cuba to America. These players include pitcher Livan Hernandez (who was the MVP of Florida's win in the 1997 World Series), shortstop Yuniesky Betancourt, and infielder Alexei Ramirez. Past Cuban-born greats include Tony Oliva, Luis Tiant, and Tony Perez.

Cummings, Candy

Although not all historians agree with the story, Candy Cummings is the 19th-century pitcher usually credited with inventing the curveball. Cummings played professionally from 1872 to 1877, and was inducted into baseball's Hall of Fame in 1939.

Cummings, whose given first name was William, packed only 120 pounds on his 5-foot 9-inch frame. Since he wasn't strong enough to blow hitters away with a fastball—in more than 2,100 career innings in the pros, he struck out only 130 batters—he developed the curveball as a teenager.

After a successful amateur career, Cummings won 124 games pitching in the National Association for four years. He joined the Hartford club in the National League's inaugural season in 1876, when he became the first man to pitch complete games (and win) both ends of a doubleheader. He played only one more season, pitching ineffectively for the Cincinnati Reds in 1877.

Curse of the Bambino

On January 3, 1920, the Boston Red Sox sold star pitcher and outfielder Babe Ruth to the American League-rival New York Yankees. The deal would haunt

■ *Cuban leader Fidel Castro poses with members of the powerful Cuban national team.*

Boston fans during an 86-year World Series drought that inspired stories of a curse on the club. The name "Curse of the Bambino" gained popularity in the 1990s, thanks to its regular use by Boston writers.

Before the deal, which was made to raise money for Boston owner Harry Frazee, the Yankees had never won a World Series; the Red Sox already had won four of them (the first World Series was played in 1903), including the 1918 Series. But the trade completely reversed the fortunes of both teams.

The Yankees would go on to become baseball's most successful franchise, with 26 World Series championships. The Red Sox not only failed to win another World Series until 2004, but they often lost their chances in heartbreaking fashion.

The Red Sox finally put the Curse of the Bambino to rest by sweeping the National League-champion St. Louis Cardinals in the 2004 World Series. In case there were any lingering doubts, though, Boston won the World Series again three years later with a sweep of the Colorado Rockies.

Curtain Call

This is when a player who has returned to the dugout—usually after an important home run—comes back out of it to acknowledge the cheers of the crowd. The practice started in live theatre, when actors who gave a particularly good performance were prompted by the audience to come from behind the curtain and take a bow.

Curveball

A curveball is the name of a pitch that breaks, or curves, away from or toward a hitter in the batter's box. For a right-handed pitcher, his curveball breaks away from a right-handed batter but toward a left-handed batter. For a left-handed pitcher, his curveball breaks toward a right-handed batter but away from a lefty.

A curveball is a much slower pitch than a pitcher's regular fastball—typically, 10

■ *This picture isn't backward, the sign is. Can you read it?*

miles (16 km) per hour slower. Sometimes, a curveball is called a "breaking ball." It is also known the "hook" and the "deuce" (because the standard catcher's signal for a curveball is usually two fingers).

Cutoff Man

The cutoff man is an infielder who takes a throw from an outfielder and relays the ball to a teammate at a base or at home plate. (Sometimes, the cutoff man is called the "relay man.")

Usually, the second baseman is the cutoff man if a ball is hit into the right-field corner or between the outfielders in right-center field. The shortstop is the cutoff man if a ball is hit into the left-field corner or between the outfielders in left-center field. Sometimes the first baseman or third baseman might act as the cutoff man on plays at the plate. Ideally, the cutoff man positions himself directly between the outfielder making the throw and the base to which he will relay the ball.

■ *Jake Peavy won the 2007 N.L. Cy Young Award.*

Cy Young Award

The Cy Young Award is presented annually to the best pitcher in both the American League and the National League. It is named for Hall-of-Famer Cy Young, who won 511 games from 1890 to 1911. Young died in 1955; one year later, baseball began awarding the trophy named in his honor. From 1956 to 1966, there was one Cy Young Award presented to the best pitcher in baseball. Since 1967, there have been separate American League Cy Young and National League Cy Young Awards.

Roger Clemens, who pitched for several teams in a 24-year career from 1984 to 2007, won a record seven Cy Young Awards.

The Places They Play

These are the ballparks (see page 22) in which each Major League team plays its home games, along with each park's seating capacity for baseball. The number listed in parentheses is the season the team began playing in the park.

American League

Team	Ballpark	City	Capacity
Baltimore Orioles	Oriole Park at Camden Yards (1992)	Baltimore, Maryland	48,262
Boston Red Sox	Fenway Park (1912)	Boston, Massachusetts	36,108
Chicago White Sox	U.S. Cellular Field (1991)	Chicago, Illinois	40,615
Cleveland Indians	Progressive Field (1994)	Cleveland, Ohio	43,345
Detroit Tigers	Comerica Park (2000)	Detroit, Michigan	40,950
Kansas City Royals	Kauffman Stadium (1973)	Kansas City, Missouri	38,030
L.A. Angels of Anaheim	Angel Stadium (1966)	Anaheim, California	45,050
Minnesota Twins	Hubert H. Humphrey Metrodome (1982)	Minneapolis, Minnesota	45,423
New York Yankees	New Yankee Stadium (2009)	New York, New York	52,325
Oakland Athletics	McAfee Coliseum (1968)	Oakland, California	48,219
Seattle Mariners	Safeco Field (1999)	Seattle, Washington	46,621
Tampa Bay Rays	Tropicana Field (1998)	St. Petersburg, Florida	45,000
Texas Rangers	Rangers Ballpark in Arlington (1994)	Arlington, Texas	49,178
Toronto Blue Jays	Rogers Centre (1989)	Toronto, Ontario, Canada	50,516

National League

Team	Ballpark	City	Capacity
Arizona Diamondbacks	Chase Field (1998)	Phoenix, Arizona	49,033
Atlanta Braves	Turner Field (1997)	Atlanta, Georgia	50,096
Chicago Cubs	Wrigley Field (1916)	Chicago, Illinois	41,160
Cincinnati Reds	Great American Ball Park (2003)	Cincinnati, Ohio	42,941
Colorado Rockies	Coors Field (1995)	Denver, Colorado	50,445
Florida Marlins	Dolphin Stadium (1993)	Miami, Florida	42,531
Houston Astros	Minute Maid Park (2000)	Houston, Texas	40,950
Los Angeles Dodgers	Dodger Stadium (1962)	Los Angeles, California	56,000

■ *The Indians play at Progressive Field. It is named, like many ballparks in the Majors, after a sponsor.*

Team	Ballpark	City	Capacity
Milwaukee Brewers	Miller Park (2001)	Milwaukee, Wisconsin	41,900
New York Mets	Citi Field (2009)	Flushing, New York	45,000
Philadelphia Phillies	Citizens Bank Park (2004)	Philadelphia, Pennsylvania	43,500
Pittsburgh Pirates	PNC Park (2001)	Pittsburgh, Pennsylvania	38,496
St. Louis Cardinals	Busch Stadium (2006)	St. Louis, Missouri	46,861
San Diego Padres	Petco Park (2004)	San Diego, California	46,000
San Francisco Giants	AT&T Park (2000)	San Francisco, California	41,503
Washington Nationals	Nationals Park (2008)	Washington, D.C.	41,888

Cy Young Award Winners

Each season, the best pitcher in each league is honored with the Cy Young Award (see page 83). Here is a complete list of the winners since the award began in 1956 (there was only one Cy Young Award winner for all of baseball from 1956 to 1966):

■ *2007: C.C. Sabathia.*

Year	Major League Baseball
1956	Don Newcombe, Brooklyn (NL)
1957	Warren Spahn, Milwaukee (NL)
1958	Bob Turley, N.Y. Yankees (AL)
1959	Early Wynn, Chicago White Sox (AL)
1960	Vern Law, Pittsburgh (NL)
1961	Whitey Ford, N.Y. Yankees (AL)
1962	Don Drysdale, L.A. Dodgers (NL)
1963	Sandy Koufax, L.A. Dodgers (NL)
1964	Dean Chance, L.A. Angels (AL)
1965	Sandy Koufax, L.A. Dodgers (NL)
1966	Sandy Koufax, L.A. Dodgers (NL)

Year	American League	National League
1967	Jim Lonborg, Boston	Mike McCormick, San Francisco
1968	Denny McLain, Detroit	Bob Gibson, St. Louis
1969	Mike Cuellar, Baltimore Denny McLain, Detroit (tie)	Tom Seaver, N.Y. Mets
1970	Jim Perry, Minnesota	Bob Gibson, St. Louis
1971	Vida Blue, Oakland	Ferguson Jenkins, Chicago Cubs
1972	Gaylord Perry, Cleveland	Steve Carlton, Philadelphia
1973	Jim Palmer, Baltimore	Tom Seaver, N.Y. Mets
1974	Catfish Hunter, Oakland	Mike Marshall, Los Angeles
1975	Jim Palmer, Baltimore	Tom Seaver, N.Y. Mets
1976	Jim Palmer, Baltimore	Randy Jones, San Diego
1977	Sparky Lyle, N.Y. Yankees	Steve Carlton, Philadelphia
1978	Ron Guidry, N.Y. Yankees	Gaylord Perry, San Diego
1979	Mike Flanagan, Baltimore	Bruce Sutter, Chicago Cubs

Year	American League	National League
1980	Steve Stone, Baltimore	Steve Carlton, Philadelphia
1981	Rollie Fingers, Milwaukee	Fernando Valenzuela, Los Angeles
1982	Pete Vuckovich, Milwaukee	Steve Carlton, Philadelphia
1983	LaMarr Hoyt, Chicago White Sox	John Denny, Philadelphia
1984	Willie Hernandez, Detroit	Rick Sutcliffe, Chicago Cubs
1985	Bret Saberhagen, Kansas City	Dwight Gooden, N.Y. Mets
1986	Roger Clemens, Boston	Mike Scott, Houston
1987	Roger Clemens, Boston	Steve Bedrosian, Philadelphia
1988	Frank Viola, Minnesota	Orel Hershiser, Los Angeles
1989	Bret Saberhagen, Kansas City	Mark Davis, San Diego
1990	Bob Welch, Oakland	Doug Drabek, Pittsburgh
1991	Roger Clemens, Boston	Tom Glavine, Atlanta
1992	Dennis Eckersley, Oakland	Greg Maddux, Chicago Cubs
1993	Jack McDowell, Chicago White Sox	Greg Maddux, Atlanta
1994	David Cone, Kansas City	Greg Maddux, Atlanta
1995	Randy Johnson, Seattle	Greg Maddux, Atlanta
1996	Pat Hentgen, Toronto	John Smoltz, Atlanta
1997	Roger Clemens, Toronto	Pedro Martinez, Montreal
1998	Roger Clemens, Toronto	Tom Glavine, Atlanta
1999	Pedro Martinez, Boston	Randy Johnson, Arizona
2000	Pedro Martinez, Boston	Randy Johnson, Arizona
2001	Roger Clemens, N.Y. Yankees	Randy Johnson, Arizona
2002	Barry Zito, Oakland	Randy Johnson, Arizona
2003	Roy Halladay, Toronto	Eric Gagne, Los Angeles
2004	Johan Santana, Minnesota	Roger Clemens, Houston
2005	Bartolo Colon, L.A. Angels of Anaheim	Chris Carpenter, St. Louis
2006	Johan Santana, Minnesota	Brandon Webb, Arizona
2007	C.C. Sabathia, Cleveland	Jake Peavy, San Diego
2008	Cliff Lee, Cleveland	Tim Lincecum, San Francisco

Read the index this way: "4:62" means Volume 4, page 62.

Major League Baseball

Here's an easy way to find your favorite teams in the volumes of this encyclopedia. The numbers after each team's name below indicate the volume and page on which the information can be found. For instance, 1:14 means Volume 1, page 14.

American League

East Division		Central Division		West Division	
Baltimore Orioles	1:24	Chicago White Sox	1:62	Los Angeles Angels of Anaheim	3:26
Boston Red Sox	1:42	Cleveland Indians	1:68	Oakland Athletics	3:80
New York Yankees	3:68	Detroit Tigers	2:8	Seattle Mariners	4:52
Tampa Bay Rays	5:6	Kansas City Royals	3:14	Texas Rangers	5:10
Toronto Blue Jays	5:16	Minnesota Twins	3:50		

National League

East Division		Central Division		West Division	
Atlanta Braves	1:18	Chicago Cubs	1:60	Arizona Diamondbacks	1:14
Florida Marlins	2:36	Cincinnati Reds	1:64	Colorado Rockies	1:74
New York Mets	3:66	Houston Astros	2:72	Los Angeles Dodgers	3:28
Philadelphia Phillies	4:8	Milwaukee Brewers	3:48	San Diego Padres	4:40
Washington Nationals	5:30	Pittsburgh Pirates	4:14	San Francisco Giants	4:42
		St. Louis Cardinals	4:38		

About the Authors

James Buckley, Jr. is the author of more than 60 books for young readers on a wide variety of topics–but baseball is his favorite thing to write about. His books include *Eyewitness Baseball, The Visual Dictionary of Baseball, Obsessed with Baseball*, and biographies of top baseball players, including Lou Gehrig. Formerly with *Sports Illustrated* and NFL Publishing, James is the president of Shoreline Publishing Group, which produced these volumes. Favorite team: Boston Red Sox.

Ted Keith was a writer for *Sports Illustrated Kids* magazine and has written several sports biographies for young readers. Favorite team: New York Yankees.

David Fischer's work on sports has appeared in many national publications, including *The New York Times, Sports Illustrated*, and *Sports Illustrated Kids*. His books include *Sports of the Times* and *Greatest Sports Rivalries*. Favorite team: New York Yankees

Jim Gigliotti was a senior editor at NFL Publishing (but he really liked baseball better!). He has written several books for young readers on sports, and formerly worked for the Los Angeles Dodgers. Favorite team: San Francisco Giants.